RANCHERO

RANCHERO

Rick Gavin

Minotaur Books ⚹ New York

RANCHERO. Copyright © 2011 by Rick Gavin. All rights reserved. Printed in the United States of America. For information, address St. Martin's Press, 175 Fifth Avenue, New York, N.Y. 10010.

www.minotaurbooks.com

Library of Congress Cataloging-in-Publication Data

Gavin, Rick.
    Ranchero / Rick Gavin.—1st ed.
        p. cm.
    ISBN 978-0-312-58318-7
    1. Repossession—Fiction.   2. Ranchero automobile—
Fiction.   3. Delta (Miss. : Region)—Fiction.   I. Title.
    PS3607.A9848R36 2011
    813'.6—dc23

                                        2011026217

First Edition: November 2011

10 9 8 7 6 5 4 3 2 1

For
David Atwell—
he knows why

RANCHERO

ONE

I met Percy Dwayne Dubois after a fashion at his Indianola house. I'd come to collect his television and was explaining to his wife that they'd gone three months delinquent on their rent-to-own installments. He eased up behind me—I heard the joists complain—to offer commentary with a shovel.

Lucky for me it was a fireplace shovel, though uncommonly stout as that sort goes, and he swung it with force enough to lay me out on the linoleum.

Since I'd enjoyed a sort of career in legitimate law enforcement, I'd met with occasion to get myself knocked on the head a time or three. I'd been dinged with assorted planking, a dinette chair, a brass shoe tree, had survived my share of semi-drunken glancing tire-iron blows, and was once deafened for

a week in Roanoke by a shemale named Varnella who caught
me square on the ear with a handbag full of what proved to be
shoplifted rice.

So I was familiar with the abrupt, iron-oxide flavor of it
all and the baleful overtures of gravity. I knew the barest of
chances to mount a survey of the kitchen floor before selecting
a spot and informing myself, "I think I'll stretch out here."

I don't believe I was ever altogether senseless. As him and
the wife were wrangling about me, I could make out what
they said. In what I preferred to believe at the time a home
economical impulse, she proposed they hack me up and pack
me off to the woods in a sack. She was kicking me all the
while she talked, poking me with her naked foot in a fashion
that suggested I was exasperating clutter.

"Let's think about the boy," he told her, and they contemplated together their son, who was sitting hard beside me in
his grimy, fragrant diaper.

The ammonia reek alone was probably keeping me awake.
He was rolling a little plastic sedan up and down my shirtfront while he burbled that way toddlers will and unfreighted
himself of drool. The wheels tickled and left me helpless
against the need to twitch and squirm, which earned me the
occasional supplemental shovel tap.

Up to this point, he could have gotten off with a month or
two in the lockup, back payments on his TV, and a spot of
contrition before a judge. But he saw fit to go, the way his sort
will, all white trash philosophical and decided the world was
stacked against him and he'd never know much of a shake.

He informed his wife there were higher-ups in the government in Jackson, most especially a fellow he'd crossed once on the attorney general's crew, who were looking to put him in Parchman any way that came to hand. So it hardly mattered what he did or how he went about it.

"I can't come out on top." He said it with that air of wan self-pity that's peculiar to humans with Pall Malls behind their ears and homemade tattoos.

Then he thumped me again and helped himself to my key ring and my wallet, and that was when his troubles got authentically underway.

By sheer chance I was driving a pristine 1969 Ranchero that my landlady had told me her dead husband, Gil, would have wanted me to drive. I'd never met Gil, but I'd seen a snapshot of him on her sideboard. It showed him wearing spotless coveralls and grimly Armor All-ing a tire. Gil looked the sort who'd probably rather have made me the loan of his liver than endure me to wheel his Ranchero out into the fallen world.

Sadly for him, his widow wasn't the sort to value a car, and worse still the woman was a relentless insister by disposition. She'd led off insisting I call her Pearl instead of Mrs. Jarvis, had insisted I park my Nova in her driveway instead of down by the curb. She routinely insisted her *Guideposts* on me directly out of her postbox and piecemeal items from Gil's wardrobe that never threatened to fit.

She was fond of some manner of alfalfa-looking green from the Sunflower Market and would always insist away about half of what she carried home. She forced on me count-less pans of desiccated box-mix brownies, the occasional bundle of tube socks from dollar-store sidewalk sales, and she even insisted a salve on me once for a rash I didn't have but she insisted the humidity would guarantee I got it.

Pearl had a son in New Orleans who lurked, as a rule, just out of insisting range. He'd swing by every now and again heading to Little Rock or Memphis. He never stayed the night or stuck around long enough for a proper meal. I once came across him on Pearl's back porch plundering through her handbag, and he shot me one of those miscreant sneers that gave his game away.

From then on, I felt an obligation to tolerate Pearl's insist-ing, a duty to serve as proxy for her boy. It was plain Pearl couldn't help herself. She insisted like most people breathe. So I decided that whatever she said I ought to take or do, I'd just go ahead for rank efficiency's sake and take or do it.

That's basically how I ended up with Gil's restored Ran-chero. My Nova had been chewing a bearing for the better part of a week, and the wheel had finally locked up the day before the fireplace shovel. As I was walking up the drive Pearl had come into the yard to insist some manner of cheesy casserole on me, and she was right in the middle of reinsist-ing I not park in the street when I let her in on my Nova's complaint.

To my surprise, Pearl told me she had a spare vehicle in the car shed. I lived above the thing and passed its grimy win-dows every day, but I'd just assumed Pearl's garage was chock full of the sort of clutter I'd spied already down in her cellar and out in her storage shack.

For Pearl's part, she drove a Buick sedan, one of those lozenge-shaped four-doors that looked extruded rather than designed. Pearl had personalized hers by dinging and bashing it in at every corner because Pearl had a way of insisting when she was behind the wheel as well.

"I can fit in there," she'd tell herself, and then demonstrate she couldn't.

So I hardly expected Pearl to open the car shed door to reveal not just an impeccably, almost clinically tidy interior but a Ranchero up on jack stands under a fitted tarp. The elastic at the bumpers had gone primarily to powder, so a couple of tugs on the canvas brought the covering away to reveal, in its full resplendence, Gil's restored vehicle. I now know the proper name for the color is calypso coral, a fairly arresting shade of tropical pink.

A Ranchero is essentially a glorified Fairlane, which never rated glorification. It's sort of a low-slung, boxy coupe in the front and a shallow truck in the back, not fit on the one end for a proper family or on the other for legitimate cargo. Consequently, the thing looked right at home elevated on jack stands, a street-legal curiosity on display. I'm sure Gil's goal had been to keep the tires from going square, but he'd also all but guaranteed the thing would go undriven.

It hardly seemed worth taking down, and I was saying as much to Pearl when she gave another yank upon Gil's tarp. One of the rotten fitted corners had gotten snagged on a bumper flange, and that tug proved enough to hinge the jack stands over all at once.

Gil's Ranchero rode them to the slab and settled on its shocks. The force disgorged a mouse that sat dazed on the cement, spat with violence from the undercarriage.

"Oh my," Pearl said. "Gil would have fussed."

I imagined him rotating in the churchyard.

I didn't make Pearl insist any further, just collected the oily kraft paper Gil had laid across the dash, reattached the battery cables, and removed the mangy shearling seat covers. Mice had come in through the heater vents and hauled off most of the fluff. I found the ignition key on the visor, set the choke half out, and the engine caught nearly straightaway.

My ancient Nova was ongoing proof I had no love for cars, but even I was stirred by the glorious baritone hum of Gil's Ranchero and a little mortified to stall the thing out after rolling about six feet onto the driveway.

Telling Pearl I needed to take it for a test drive, I grew capable in a block or so, and was altogether seduced before I was a full half mile from the house. The low rumble of the engine. The extra-stiff ride. The unexpected pep. The polished walnut gearshift knob that felt erotic in my hand. My Nova had fluttering heat shields and wallowing suspension, clattering valves that made the thing sound like a Pacific Rim sweatshop on wheels.

Once I'd returned to the house and parked the thing, I pledged an oath to Pearl about the scrupulous care I'd take of Gil's Ranchero. I assured her that I'd bring it back exactly like

I'd found it, which is the statement I fixed on as I lay sprawled on that gritty kitchen floor.

Just before they left, that boy and his wife had tied me up with lamp cord, had given me one last shovel swat in the face, and shoved me under their dinette. Because they were shiftless trash, I was almost half a minute working loose, and I gained my feet by hauling myself slowly up a chair.

I could see my face in the breakfront glass. I was lumpy and puffy and crimson with my nose laid open along the bridge and my left eye swollen shut. My bottom lip was split. I'd leaked a slurry of bloody drool on my shirtfront. I had a headache of the blinding and unperforated sort.

I'd heard them start up Gil's Ranchero, so I knew it'd be gone from the drive. They'd left me their rust-eaten Pacer with a screwdriver plunged in a sidewall, the best they could manage by way of forestalling pursuit.

The front room was shin-deep in trash and pieces of cast-off clothing. A ratty couch, a corner cupboard full of mismatched cups and saucers, and a dying aspidistra in a shiny plastic pot. They'd taken, of course, their plasma TV, the very thing I'd come to fetch.

I should have called my boss straightaway. That was company protocol. Whenever one of us got in a dustup, K-Lo insisted we phone him—not so he could help us out, but more so he could rant and fume. K-Lo was a hothead by disposition and technique, and there was little in this life he preferred to righteous indignation.

His given name was Kalil, and he was Lebanese by descent.

His parents sold kibbe and *domas* from a storefront up in Clarksdale. K-Lo's great grandfather had come to the Mississippi Delta to farm.

When the slaves were freed and the planters had liberated their field hands, they went scouring the planet for labor to help harvest the cotton crop. They brought in nearly anybody they could persuade to come. Italians, Slovaks, Asians, Africans, Mexicans, Middle Easterners—people in desperate enough straits back home to find the Delta inviting.

Of course, it turned out that picking cotton by hand in the Mississippi sun was precisely the sort of work you had to be indentured to do. If you thought you were miserable in Naples, Dubrovnik, Hunang, Rabat, or Damascus, you'd reconsider after a week in a Delta cotton patch.

Consequently, most immigrants gave up farming, but they stayed on nonetheless, could hardly afford to just pick up and leave. They became shopkeepers and tinkerers, money lenders and levee builders; opened stalls and restaurants to sell the food they'd eaten back home. That's why there's falafel in Clarksdale, congee in Greenville, tamales all over the place. Stuck smack in the middle of the homogenous South, the Delta is crazy exotic.

As a rule, deepest Dixie is black and white and Christian in a way the Lord and Savior could never have intended. Your basic Southern Baptist would willingly delay his personal ascent into heaven for the baser pleasure of hanging around to see you burn in hell. The Delta just supplies a regional wrinkle in the common tone.

K-Lo's people might have been Muslim, but they'd evolved to the Southern veneer. They drank sweet tea, wore Walmart denim, and could rattle on about the weather, but they'd all retained their Middle Eastern volatility. It was an unrelenting tribal trait like being towheaded or chinless. I knew if I dialed up K-Lo, he'd effectively explode.

I decided instead to call Desmond, a far more temperate soul and the only one of my colleagues I liked. Unfortunately, I'd left my Motorola on the dash of the Ranchero and couldn't locate anything but vacant phone jacks in the house, which sent me outside to waylay a boy on a bike down by the street. He didn't see me until I was right beside him, when he all but levitated.

"Shit, mister!" he yelped, and retreated across the road in an awful hurry. It took a five-dollar bill to lure him back so I could rent his phone. He studied me while I dialed up Desmond to tell him where I was. Desmond didn't ask questions, just agreed he'd come and fetch me.

"What happened to you?" the boy wanted to know once I'd handed his phone back to him.

"I got in a tussle," I told him, and jabbed my thumb at the house I'd come out of. "Know him?"

He nodded. "Daddy says he stole our mower." Then he added by way of friendly advice, "You might want to work on your tussling."

TWO

While I waited for Desmond to roll up, I rooted through the house and found that fireplace shovel on the floor in the half bath. By way of tussling practice, I attacked the corner cupboard and pulverized every mismatched dish I could reach.

Given the heft of the pan, I had to think that if that boy had swatted me in earnest, I'd have been a candidate for the mortuary. I was lucky in the end he was the type to do everything half-assed.

My headache finally overcame me, and I fished some ice out of the freezer that I wrapped in a purple tube top the wife had left on the dinette. I parked out on the front steps and applied the thing to my welts and contusions while I waited for Desmond to work his way over to me from the Sonic.

He'd been eating a Coney Island when I reached him on the phone, and I well knew there wasn't any chance of rushing him along.

Desmond was methodical and maddeningly meticulous, took a glacial approach to every little thing he did. He'd gotten shot once in a roadhouse fight and had driven himself to the hospital in Greenville, where he'd nearly bled to death while trying to park snug to the curb. But I knew I could depend on Desmond to show up even if only at length, and the Delta is a place where you can't, as a rule, depend on anything much.

Desmond had gone through an ugly divorce about a year before I met him, ugly for him, anyway, but productive for his ex. She'd gotten their house in Ruleville along with Desmond's Escalade, and while he might have been happy to be done with her, he'd mourned the loss of his Caddy.

Desmond had loved his Escalade and had spent a small fortune on rims. Now his ex went flying around in the thing and didn't even wash it. Worse still, in the settlement Desmond had gotten his ex's Geo Metro, which Desmond, given his size, was obliged to drive from the backseat.

I'd once been in Desmond's company when we'd run across his ex out in the parking lot of the Pecan House. She was a wee thing—all stick-on nails and hair extensions and palpable bad faith. She was with a fellow she kept calling her "intended," some lowlife from Chicago in a faux-silk shirt who wore a soul patch that would have embarrassed a goat.

Talk turned quickly to money Desmond's ex had convinced herself he owed her, which her "intended" got right on the verge of volunteering a remark about. Then he noticed how Desmond and I were looking at him.

I could smell the outstanding warrants that had chased him from Illinois, and I knew Desmond was hoping to meet with cause to fling him to the pavement and kick him around the parking lot for a while.

Desmond's ex, Shawnica, rattled off a litany of reasons why Desmond owed her two hundred and sixty-seven dollars. It had something to do with a power bill and a revolving department store charge, but Desmond was fixed on his Escalade sitting behind her and didn't seem to hear.

The front end was bug-encrusted, and the windows were all greasy and smudged. A shroud of brake dust had dulled the elaborate faceted chrome of the rims.

As Shawnica nattered on about her needs and Desmond's obligations, I could see that Desmond was working toward some manner of eruption. To the untrained eye, it wouldn't have looked like anything at all. Desmond was a little too blubbered over for telltale signs of emotion, but I'd been around him enough by then to read him fairly well.

The slight squint, the snort, the way he closed and opened his monstrous hands as Shawnica aired her grievances and tallied up her charges. I had the sense to take a full step back.

Seconds thereafter, Desmond punched the intended in the sternum, and him and his soul patch went flying like they'd been fired from a circus canon. That boy landed on the trunk of a Camry in a sleazy, groaning pile while Desmond turned and lumbered toward his Geo.

Shawnica was just behind him in a comprehensive rage. He swung open the driver's door and went about fitting himself inside while Shawnica screeched and slapped at Desmond with her open hands until all of her stick-on nails had broken loose and fallen off. They lay like so much glittering litter on the pavement.

Desmond hauled on his seat belt, adjusted his rearview mirror ever so slightly, and started his engine as he reached his elbow to lock his door. Shawnica couldn't smack him hard enough to make him act like she was there.

"Come on, Nick," he told me, so I climbed in and we rolled across the lot with Shawnica running beside us all the while.

She was simultaneously smacking Desmond and shrieking for the law. We were a good thirty yards up the truck route before we managed to leave her behind. Even then she pulled a shoe off and flung it at us.

Desmond drove directly to the Sonic for a couple of Coney Islands. If Desmond had a bat cave, the Indianola Sonic was it. A city cruiser came by while Desmond was busy marshaling condiments. It eased up beside us with a couple of cracker cops inside.

Just as the near one was asking us about the punched intended, Desmond shifted around and drew him up short with a glance.

Desmond could be menacing. He was huge and eggplant

black and had a way of looking feral when he wanted. The
chances must have seemed good, even to pinhead crackers
with badges, that Desmond might be trouble to bring in. The
cop who'd been talking simply shut up, and the one behind
the wheel dropped the cruiser into gear and drove out of the
Sonic just like he'd driven in.

"Damn, Obi-Wan," I said in an admiring sort of way, and
Desmond uncorked what passed with him for laughter. It
sounded like somebody sneezing from the far end of a culvert.
Then he punched me fondly in the arm, and I bounced off the
passenger door.

After that day, Desmond would do for me and I would do
for him, and we didn't have to say a thing about it.

So I might have waited an hour, but I knew Desmond
would show at last, and he finally rolled up and made a minor career out of parking curbside. I watched him from the
porch steps with my fireplace shovel in hand as he fought his
way out of his Geo like a man scrabbling out of a hole.

"Who done that?" he asked me.

I hadn't suspected I'd look a fright from the street. I jabbed
my thumb toward the house behind me. "Some boy. Can't say
who yet."

"What with?" Desmond wanted to know.

I smacked the porch rail with that shovel. The steel pan
rang out deep and pure.

"Lord, Nick," Desmond told me. "You just might ought
to be dead."

THREE

Burglary is a going career in the Mississippi Delta, and K-Lo's rental shop had been broken into a half dozen times or more. One of the last batches of thieves had carried off K-Lo's stuffed catamount not two months back. It had been posed on a rock primed to pounce with its red lacquered tongue sticking out. Kalil had killed it himself, which he was usually pleased to mention in part. He routinely left out the bit about how he'd hit it with his Civic.

The theft of that cat had gotten entirely under Kalil's skin, and he'd gone out in a righteous rage and bought himself a Beretta shotgun. His plan was to lay for the next thieving bastards and rain some vengeance on them.

Of course, a shotgun doesn't pair so well with a hothead

like Kalil, so we took it as our common duty to keep the thing unloaded. Kalil would get in a snit and shove shells in, and we'd slip around and eject them, for selfish reasons as much as anything else.

Even a calm, careful man who fires a shotgun in a store full of televisions is likely to take out a Panasonic or three. Kalil, we feared, might shoot us all straight into unemployment.

We figured he was better off yelling, and he could be brutal with a tirade. I saw K-Lo lay waste to a fellow maybe a week after he'd hired me, an ex-con named Ronnie who unboxed freight and drove a panel truck.

Ronnie had gone out on a delivery and caught his mirror on a light pole. He'd confessed as much to Kalil straightaway and had offered to pay for the damage, but Kalil had gone off on him nonetheless. He did a devastating job of poking Ronnie in his rawest places. Ronnie was a hapless fuckup, so there was plenty to exploit, and K-Lo managed in maybe ninety seconds to mount a scathing history of Ronnie's abiding talent for benighted misadventure.

That was the first time I had ever seen a tattooed felon weep.

Happily, K-Lo's wife would swing by the store a couple of times a week to lavish a little ungoverned abuse on K-Lo.

Their marriage had been arranged. K-Lo had carried the woman from Beirut to a Leland ranch house on a fly-blown bayou, so she'd given up the Paris of the Middle East for the ancestral home of Kermit the Frog. She seemed to resent it a little more bitterly with each passing day.

She liked to stop in and remind Kalil of all the Delta hardships she'd never have known if she'd just stayed back home in Lebanon. She seemed to prefer to do it at peak volume.

They'd rage at each other throughout the store, no matter who was about. K-Lo would dip into the stockroom, and his wife would follow him, shrieking. They'd have alfresco screaming matches on the slab by the loading ramp. The ordeal had a way of deflating Kalil, and he'd be spent for the balance of the day.

I happened to get beat with that fireplace shovel while K-Lo's wife was away. She'd been up in Brooklyn for a week already visiting assorted cousins, so K-Lo had been raging unchecked for days and had gathered a vile head of steam. When me and Desmond pulled into the shopping plaza lot, he was out on the sidewalk smoking.

"Where's my goddamn TV?" he barked my way, letting it serve as well for "you look like shit" and "hello."

"They took it," I said. "Hit me with this." I held up my fireplace shovel.

K-Lo spat with disgust and drew his cigarette down to the filter in a spasm of rage. Then he flicked his butt and bounced it off my shirtfront. It exploded in sparks and fell to the pavement, where I ground it out with my boot.

"Hey!" K-Lo shouted, and his right hand, Patty, came scampering out of the store. "Get Dale," he told her.

Dale was a raging psychopath and Patty's husband both at once. He was a county policeman, a bigot, a misogynist, a xenophobe, and a musclehead who appeared to live on supplements and Skoal. Dale had developed so much veiny bulk in his years of hoisting dumbbells that it had reached the point where he could hardly fit in his uniform. He was all chiseled contours and looked like he'd walked straight out of a Marvel Comic.

K-Lo liked to call him in when customers defaulted because Dale was the sort of cop who lived to beat civilians up.

Patty ran into the store to phone him. Even from out in the parking lot we could hear every word she told Dale because he was a tireless plinker who thought earplugs were for faggots, so he'd made of himself a burly heterosexual who couldn't hear shit.

Apparently he was over on the truck route making trouble for a pack of Mexicans. It seems Dale had pulled them for too damn much tread wear and was turning their car inside out. It should be said that Dale thought anybody who spoke Spanish was a Mexican, and it took only two of them together to constitute a pack.

So as far as anybody knew, Dale might have been hassling a dozen unpapered migrants or engineering an ugly forenoon for the king and queen of Spain. Either way, it was plain Dale thought he might be tied up for a bit, and I figured we might have twenty minutes to get what we needed from K-Lo. This was all my business, and I didn't want the pair of them muck-ing it up—Dale with his blundering stupidity and K-Lo with his scattershot rage.

"I'll want paper on that boy," I told K-Lo, and he bolted straightaway, running headlong into the store like we wouldn't know where to find him.

Desmond and I followed him back to his office. We gave him the chance to unbolt his door before Desmond bucked against it once and blew it off its hinges. The thing hit K-Lo and knocked the shotgun from his hands. I stood on the barrel to keep him from picking it up.

"Paper," I said, and K-Lo looked like he might just vomit on me.

When it came to the details of his business, K-Lo was clinically unwell. He couldn't bring himself to let anybody know anything at all. We never went out on repos with actual invoices in hand but just scraps from a pad where K-Lo'd written a physical address. He wouldn't even give us the customers' names because he lived in nagging fear we'd go all devious and entrepreneurial on him.

"PAPER," I insisted, and K-Lo stood there stricken and forlorn until Desmond bent him over his desk and applied sufficient tonnage to tempt K-Lo to reorder what he cared about and why. Breathing moved up to the top of the list and paperwork drifted well south.

K-Lo pulled a tissuey pink invoice from a file in a desk drawer and then held to it so I had to snatch it from him.

"Hear that?" Desmond asked me.

It was an approaching siren on full *WA-WA*, Dale's preference for getting cars the hell out of his way.

"Shit," I said, and me and Desmond legged it through the store.

We reached the parking lot just as Dale came wheeling off the truck route. He passed breakneck through the gutter and nearly left his muffler there. I had to guess Patty had called him back more than a little frantic, and sure enough Dale had just thrown his Mexicans into the back of his car.

I didn't have a clear idea of precisely what I'd do until Dale whipped in beside me and loomed up out of his cruiser. He laid one hand to the hilt of his Ruger and grabbed his toothpick with the other.

"What the shit's going on?" Dale asked me at a volume fit for cattle drives. All I had was K-Lo's pink tissuey invoice and that fireplace shovel.

I well knew there was no explaining anything to Dale. He'd not been designed and constructed for cogitation. I glanced at the woman and her three weeping children shut up in the squalid backseat where Dale usually hauled around meth heads and drunks whenever Mexicans weren't handy.

A two-fisted backhand seemed called for, a looping Björn Borgish sort of thing. I caught Dale just above his right ear with the flat of that shovel pan. If his head had detached, it would have been heavy with topspin. The steel rang so loudly that those three Mexican children stopped crying at once.

All of us watched Dale teeter for about a quarter minute before his lower half decided it couldn't support his upper bulk. He went down with stately deliberation, like a punctured ocean liner. I shoved a foot under his head to keep it from bouncing off of the pavement.

There was blood, of course, where Dale's scalp had parted cleanly from the blow. It spouted and flowed so extravagantly that Patty went a little daft, and I had to take Dale's pistol from her before she could shoot me with it. Then I flung open the back door of the cruiser and told Dale's Mexicans, *"Adios."* It did the job, judging by how they scrambled.

"Not quite the day I'd hoped for," I said once I'd met Desmond at the Geo. "Sure you want to do this?"

Desmond told me, "Doing it already."

FOUR

Of course, Desmond needed a Coney Island just to settle his nerves, but we both doubted he could Obi-Wan us out of this mess, so we passed up the Indianola Sonic for the branch on the outskirts of Greenville, twenty miles west, and backed up to the Mississippi River.

We got takeout and carried it over the levee to a weedy, trash-strewn park with a view of a flooded cottonwood grove and a derelict casino barge.

By then I'd studied K-Lo's invoice and knew what we were up against. That boy wasn't just a shithead with a shovel anymore. He was a Dubois, a name they couldn't be bothered to Frenchify in the Delta. *Dew*-boys—front loaded and hick specific—was good enough for them.

Duboises were notorious unprincipled rubbish, and the region was filthy with them. That boy could have been an O'Malley in Dublin for all the sifting we'd have to do.

"Percy Dwayne," I said, reading it out. "Know him?"

Desmond shook his head. He drew open his shirt at the collar to show me a leathery scar on his shoulder. "Luther Dubois, down by Yazoo." Desmond said. "Him," he told me, "I know."

Desmond had a buddy, Kendell, who was reliable police. He'd worked all over the Delta, from Clarksdale clear to Vicksburg, and was always getting laid off and rehired as the books and the budgets permitted. The last Desmond had heard, he was doing traffic stops out in Leflore County.

There's a spa hotel in Greenwood people come to for a treat, and the bulk of them get there on Route 7 off the interstate, through Leflore County. Like most Delta roads, it's flat and straight, and you've hit ninety before you know it. A vindictive lawman can empty a summons book in an afternoon.

"Kendell's got no use for Dale," Desmond told me. "Might help us run that Dubois down."

We were soon back in the Geo driving though downtown Greenville. It's a hard place to be inconspicuous because there's nobody much around, and Greenville's a town that was grand once and sprawling and overrun with people. The boulevards are wide. The vacant buildings are ornate, Romanesque piles. When steamboats still called and cotton left the Delta on the river, Greenville had an opera house and a full-time chamber orchestra. It had hotels and restaurants and ladies' boutiques, was invested with cachet and bustle, which had all drained away well past the point of exhaustion over the years.

Now Greenville had empty storefronts and intermittent renewal projects that never got beyond bricking the crosswalks and changing out the lampposts.

There were a couple of cars parked slant in at the diner near the levee, but otherwise the place was desolate except for me and Desmond. Anybody looking for two fellows in a Geo could have seen us from three hundred yards away.

Desmond chose to dodge the truck route on a back way out of Greenville that would loop through open farmland and bring us to Highway 7 after a while. The road we were on had been house-lined at first and then shack-plagued and hovel-dotted before we passed beyond people entirely into an unbroken sea of green.

We went from weeds and trash and leggy gardenia bushes and drowsy mongrels to luxurious jade green soybeans stretching as far as we could see. The transition was stark and instructive, a sort of Delta affirmation that the people could go to shit if they pleased, but the crops would go to market.

We'd rolled in an instant out of food stamps and into agribusiness. There might have been chicken fingers and government cheese for the two-legged fauna, but the flora would get no end of what it needed to survive. Bug spray and herbicide. Fertilizer and irrigation. Seed engineered to make the plants impervious to Mississippi.

There wasn't much on this earth that could touch a mod-

ern Delta crop if the ag school in Starkville had decided it
was better off unbothered.

The soybeans eventually yielded to rice. The rice gave way
to wheat. The wheat was eclipsed at last by several thousand
acres of corn, all of it over head-high and meticulously level. A
red crop duster, an Ag Cat, was flying back and forth dousing
that corn with something. It banked steeply over the road as
we passed beneath it and doused us a little as well.

Time and ingenuity had drained the heartbreak out of
Delta farming. It was primarily about money now. If you
could buy the land, afford the seed, the tractors and the diesel,
pay for the chemicals and the poly pipe, hire the dusters and
the combines, you were all but sure to realize what the market
would allow along with what the government would subsi-
dize.

These days a man could run a ten-thousand-acre Delta
spread with a handful of tractor drivers and the odd combine
operator, which left most everybody else with little or nothing to do.

You could work in a catfish plant, but those jobs came
and went with the price of feed. You might find some hourly
clerking job in a box store on the truck route, catch on at the
Long John Silver or repossess TVs, supplement your monthly
government check with scattershot larceny. Or you could do
what the bulk of people had done and simply pack up and
leave.

As a guy who's spent his share of time knocking around

the South, I've never come across a place as empty as the Delta, and it's double desolate because the towns are still standing but the people are mostly gone. The folks remaining either couldn't afford to sell off and get out or were comfortable enough already so they could stay no matter what.

The place would probably be better off razed with every arable acre plowed under. The soil is black and loamy, tailormade for agriculture, so it'd be smarter to let the people congregate around the edges and give John Deere and Allis-Chalmers the general run of the place.

Life in the Delta demands sweet-tea existentialism, a view of the world narcotic at bottom and sugared over with courtliness. Heat and mosquitoes in summer. Scouring wind in winter. Anemic prospects lingering through the year. People steal and drink. They work when they can, get along as best they're able, and the mood of the place extends to the local police as well. Except for fools like Dale, no lawman in the Delta ever gets too terribly worked up. Such a wealth of civilians about are given to rampant shiftlessness that a cop with his gun out would find himself faced with too damn many people to shoot.

I was still new to the place, maybe eight months in, and hadn't fully acclimated. I wasn't yet used to driving an hour and a half to get anywhere I needed to be, hadn't acquired a taste for Kool-Aid pickles or venison tamales, wasn't entirely at ease as part of the puny white minority.

I was getting there, but I'd spent my last decade in the eastern Virginia uplands, working as Deputy Nick Reid in the middle of nowhere much. The hillbillies up there had come by their parsimony from Scotland, their marksmanship from Daddy and Daniel Boone, and their dunderheaded obliviousness from taking cousins for wives.

They didn't have any manners, barely had language I could understand, and seemed to live for hunting out of season and beating each other up. I'd passed the bulk of my time sorting out the same couple of dozen people until their children came of age for proper charges when I got to sort them, too. I don't think I did an ounce of good the whole time I was up there, and once the job had brought out the Dale in me, I'd had the sense to quit.

I'd lit in the Delta because I could tell it was something else altogether with terrain about as far from Virginia hillbilly hollows as I could get. Everything was slower and hotter, the local manners approached baroque, and racing down a Delta road with crop dusters on the horizon was like driving into 1952.

The Delta was otherworldly, even for folks in the rest of Mississippi who'd explain away outlandishness that transpired in the Delta by shrugging and saying, "It ain't like nowhere else."

The place had a reputation for the natives living a little too close to the ground. The black trash was trashier than in normal Mississippi. The Delta crackers were capable of almost any enormity sober and everything otherwise once they'd gotten drunk.

The Delta had its own rules, its own peculiar customs.

There were people in the Delta who'd help you out for no
conceivable reason and people who'd extract your vital organs
for sport. I'd hardly begun to understand the whys and where-
fores of the place, which made Desmond indispensable to me.
He was my guide to all things Mississippi flatland. I had need
of Delta insight and Delta education, and Desmond was my
personal lyceum.

He never played the radio when he was behind the wheel
of his Geo. Instead he whistled through his teeth and drifted
all over the road. Steering never seemed to hold much lasting
interest for Desmond. He preferred pointing out silos and
telling tales of various farms he'd worked on back when he
could fit in a tractor seat.

There were squashed armadillos all over the place putre-
fying in the sun, and given the way we wandered we rarely
failed to hit a carcass. Consequently, the ride out to Highway
7 was perfumed with rancid meat and what I'd grown to
think of as eau de W. R. Grace—a tangy chemical nosebleed
aroma that was the signature scent of the place.

We found Kendell backed in a slot between two cypress
trees. I'd met him on a repo that had soured on me on a couple
of months before. I was trying to get payment from a covey of
Klinnards when the whole thing had gone sideways.

They'd fallen to fighting each other—the entire crew—
and we were in their trailer at the time. They were all Delta
fat, about Desmond's size but too full of beer to be lively, so
they'd just laid on each other and described the thrashings
they'd inflict if they could.

One of them got squashed so thoroughly that he passed out in the doorway and so trapped me and the rest of his clan inside. That's when I put in the 9-1-1 that Kendell responded to.

I watched him out a window as he exited his cruiser and pepper-sprayed all the mongrels that came snarling up to meet him. Kendell lay against that trailer door while I pulled it from inside, and we made a gap that Kendell could slip in through.

He wasn't hungry for particulars. Kendell just drew out his lacquered nightstick and went about tapping Klinnard bony parts. It earned him undivided Klinnard attention.

Kendell was from Tchula and knew his Delta crackers inside out. Duboises would have ganged up on him and fought him to the death. They're pretty much the Gurkhas of the region, but Klinnards are more like the Vichy French and don't have any steel to speak of.

"You going to pay this man?" Kendell asked, and all those Klinnards pledged they would.

Two of them made the mistake of swearing on their mother's grave, their mother who Kendell knew to be sitting in jail in Alabama, so he swatted those boys once further in righteous exasperation before advising them all to scratch up the cash due on their TV.

They came within thirteen dollars of everything they owed, and I was quick to let it go at that so I could follow Kendell out.

I squeezed behind him through the door gap and down

the rickety cinder-block steps into the landfill that passed with those Klinnards for a yard. The dogs all shied and cowered as Kendell made way to his cruiser with me trailing close and prattling out of nerves and gratitude.

When I finally shut up, Kendell volunteered one thing alone. "These goddamn people," he told me, "make me tired."

Out on 7, Desmond parked by a sorghum patch on the far side of the cruiser.

He called out to Kendell, "Hey here." He told him, "I guess you'll be wanting Dale's gun."

Kendell said, "I suppose." He looked a little weary to see us.

Kendell had heard all about us on the scanner. Desmond told him, "Wasn't nothing we planned."

"Hell, boys, I hope not," Kendell said as he climbed out of his cruiser.

Kendell was, if anything, blacker than Desmond and hard everywhere Desmond was soft. We all leaned on the cruiser fender while Kendell told us what he'd heard. That Dale was at the hospital getting his head sewn up. That me and Desmond were the ones behind it. That there were proper warrants sworn out but no push much to enforce them since nobody—except Patty—gave a happy goddamn about Dale.

"The gun'll help," Kendell allowed, and then studied me a little. "What the hell," he finally asked me, "happened to you."

"A Dubois beat me with a shovel."

Kendell snorted by way of suggesting I was rigorously full of shit. "A Dubois would have put you in the ground."

I unfolded K-Lo's pink invoice and handed it to Kendell. I knew he knew it was as reliable as an affidavit given K-Lo's anal approach to his clientele. K-Lo's customers may have been lowlives, but he made it his special business to know precisely which lowlives they were.

"Hmm," Kendell said as he studied the thing. "Percy Dwayne Dubois." Then he gazed toward the tree line—over the Metro and out past the sorghum patch—while he ran through his mental catalog of Duboises he'd run up on until he'd settled on a candidate or three.

"Drives a Wrangler?"

I shook my head, and Desmond added helpfully, "Weren't but a fireplace shovel."

Kendell surveyed me once further. "Pacer. Back left fender rusted through."

"That's him," I said.

Kendell ran a finger of one hand across the knuckles of the other. "Tats?" he said. "Little fellow? Blond?"

I nodded.

With that he laid his hand out maybe four feet off the ground. "About this tall?" Kendell winked at Desmond and then smiled at me as if to suggest my Dubois had been a gay dwarf hanger-on.

"The shovel might have been small, but the Dubois wasn't. I'll be happy to tap you with it?"

"Should have seen what it did to Dale," Desmond said, and Kendell allowed he wished he had.

He'd pulled that Dubois and his wife over a few times for

a variety of infractions. Or rather he'd stopped them for speeding and then had piled on the citations afterward. Driving once without a hood. Once with three stolen car seats and a pair of plundered strollers. Once with that baby of theirs on the dashboard to make room for his daddy's bong.

"Caught them doing eighty riding through here on two donuts. She was driving and didn't stop until we'd blocked the road at Holcombe. He's bad," Kendell said, "but that wife of his, she'll do any damn thing."

I caught myself wondering how close I'd come to getting chopped up into bits.

Kendell told us she was a Vardaman, which prompted Desmond to groan. The only Vardaman I'd ever heard of was the Mississippi senator who'd called Teddy Roosevelt a coonflavored miscegenationist to his face.

"One of that brood," Kendell assured me, "from over in the hills by Okolona."

Then Desmond and Kendell threw in together to make me understand there were people about in the Delta who'd migrated to the place because the folks back where they'd come from weren't malicious enough to suit them.

The Delta was home still to pockets of ignorant misfits and temperamental throwbacks, Confederates to the marrow fueled by white-hot resentments and sustained by bigotry. It seemed that Dubois's wife had come to the Delta to be among her own the way some people move to Berkeley or to Paris.

"Where do you think they'd go?" I asked Kendell.

"Give them a week or two. They'll turn up."

That's when I acquainted Kendell with the calypso coral Ranchero that was keeping me from sitting by and waiting for them to surface again.

"I swore," I told him, "I'd bring it back just like I drove it off."

Kendell, to his credit, just said, "All right," and then turned and informed Desmond, "I stopped him two or three weeks ago with Luther in the car."

Desmond's hand moved automatically to the scar on his left shoulder.

"You might find him and that wife of his down around Yazoo," Kendell said. "Even those two might have the sense to stay off the roads in a pink Ranchero."

The whole time we'd been standing there talking, the drivers up on Highway 7 had been trying to slow from ninety to sixty immediately and at once. The sight of the cruiser was all it took, as a general rule, anyway, until a boy in a beat-up Dodge pickup shot by us without braking.

Kendell tended to take that sort of behavior as a provocation, so he told me and Desmond, "Watch out," and jumped into his car. He went sailing up onto the pavement with his grille lights strobing and raced out of sight.

"New Sonic down at Yazoo," Desmond told me. "Haven't tried it yet."

"Aren't they all the same?"

Desmond glared at me like the pope himself might stare down Satan's minion.

We waited for Kendell to come back because it seemed

the courteous thing to do, but we were a good half hour standing around before he eased down off of the roadway.

"These damn people," Kendell said once he'd backed into his slot.

He climbed out of his cruiser and circled around to open his trunk. Kendell lifted out a feed sack and set it on the ground. It was so alive with movement that me and Desmond were retreating before Kendell had even begun to unknot the neck.

"Taking them to his ex-wife's boyfriend's house. Going to put them in his bathtub or somewhere."

With that, Kendell dumped probably eight or ten writhing cottonmouths onto the ground. Somehow Desmond levitated onto the cruiser hood, and his bulk transformed an upswept contour into a sizable divot. I perched on the quarter panel and lifted my feet off of the ground.

I don't care for snakes as a rule, but moccasins are particularly unnerving because there's no sign of the Lord's work about them to admire. They're silt-colored and unpatterned, plump and short; seem like ungainly, venomous miscalculations.

Desmond's objections were more in the vein that they were simply loose reptiles. The panicked noises he made while scaling the windshield were like nothing I'd ever heard from a human.

Kendell tried everything short of pulling his service revolver to get us down and ended up having to ferry us to a patch of snakeless hardpan, where I hopped off the fender while Desmond lingered near the roof.

"They're just snakes," Kendell told us, which might as well have been, "Hell, boys, it's only plutonium," for all the good it did us to hear it said.

Even once we'd lured him down on the hardpan, Desmond couldn't keep from watching the ground, which prompted Kendell to ask us both, with a touch of wonderment, "So you two are going after a Dubois?"

Then Desmond tapped me on the arm and pointed at his Geo, down between the sorghum patch and Kendell's cyprus trees, where the grass was ripe with reptiles and about knee deep.

"Key's in it," he told me.

FIVE

I'd not yet made it down to Yazoo City, so this was a fresh trip for me, but it tracked pretty close to all of my other excursions in the Delta. Lots of crops, a few shacks and trailers, the occasional brick villa in a pasture, and every now and again an authentic plantation left from olden days.

There wasn't much cotton under cultivation. Desmond said there was a glut and the price was ungodly low, but we passed almost no end of soybeans and staggering fields of corn.

Desmond told me the ears went to Arkansas cattle and the stalks to biofuel. Then he pointed at a silo back off the road on a farm he'd worked before he'd gotten husky. When Desmond talked about his bulk, that was the word he always used.

I had to pivot around to even find him in that Geo. He'd made a kind of fainting couch out of the driver's seat, had shoved it well back off the rails and was all but reclining with his feet on the pedals and his head in the rear window well. It was like he was a row behind me at the cineplex.

"Tell me about Luther," I said, but Desmond pointed instead to a grain bin and went on at some length about a combine driver he'd known.

I don't think Desmond missed farming so much as he missed being tractor-seat sized. I doubt it was all hot dogs that did him in. Desmond was doomed to be gigantic, and once the fieldwork had dried up, there wasn't much for him to do but sit around and swell.

His sister was huge. His father had been massive, and Desmond's mother was so doughy and weak on her pins that she hardly ever left her bed. I'd met her once. Her tiny head had been sticking out of a heap of blankets in her stifling bedroom. She was wearing some kind of elaborate wig with bangs and braided bits, and she must have tossed it on to receive me because the thing was a little cockeyed.

"And Luther?" I asked Desmond when the combine talk was done, but before he could speak his phone rang. Well, it didn't ring exactly. It played a snatch of Barry White's "Satin Soul" and then played it three or four times more before Desmond could dig the thing out of his shirt pocket and look to see who was calling.

He tossed his phone my way. "It's you," he told me.

It was, in fact, my Motorola ringing Desmond up. I didn't

quite know what to say when I answered, so I said just, "Yel-low."

"Who's this?" that Dubois asked me.

"Who you looking for?"

"I got him," that Dubois fairly howled in the direction, I guess, of his wife. Then he came back my way and said, "We've been calling all your numbers. Nobody gives a shit about you."

"I'm coming for you, asshole."

He went half to pieces laughing. "Where you coming?"

"I'll find you," I told him. "Don't you worry about that."

"Then I guess you're wanting your truck thing back? It's a hell of a pretty ride, but I can be convinced to hand it over."

"I'm listening," I said.

"Going to cost you five thousand," that Dubois told me. "Did I tell you it's a hell of a pretty ride?"

"I think you did."

I didn't say anything for about a half minute, which Percy Dwayne didn't much care for.

"So?" he said, and when I still didn't say anything, he said it again. "So?"

"That's a lot of money."

"Not for this beauty."

"Let's say I pay it. How's this going to happen?"

"Twenties," he said, and instructed me to drop the cash the following day at noon at an address up in Webb. "Put it in the mail slot," he told me.

"Five thousand in twenties? That won't fit in any damn mail slot."

"Then put it in a bag on the porch," he said. "Just put it some damn where."

"What about the car?"

"You'll get it," he told me, "once I have the money."

Desmond was drifting so that he hit an armadillo in the middle of the oncoming lane. It was ripe and greasy, and I feared for a second we'd spin into the ditch. Even Desmond stopped whistling and cut loose with a "Shit howdy."

"I don't know," I told Percy Dwayne. "This world's full of cars."

"Well," he said, "you'll pay me or you won't."

"Can't argue with you there."

"Figure it out and call me in an hour." And with that he started rattling off his number.

"It's my number, moron. I know it already."

Percy Dwayne swore a little further and hung up.

"They all this dumb?" I asked Desmond.

He nodded. "It's the mean mixed in that's the problem."

Desmond didn't care for the Yazoo City Sonic. The burger I ate tasted like all the burgers I'd ever had at a Sonic, and Desmond's Coney Islands looked true to form. But Desmond found the chili slightly thin and under-seasoned, and he thought the Yazoo Sonic was poorly situated as Sonics go.

Given that the natural Sonic habitat is peripheral retail clottage, an unscenic Sonic is bound to be a relative kind of thing. Desmond's trouble was he couldn't find a parking space to suit him. The Yazoo Sonic was set back off the road and boasted an unobstructed view of the backside of the neighboring shopping plaza, so all we had to look at were overflowing Dumpsters and steel security doors.

"A fence wouldn't hurt," Desmond said, and added beyond it, "Salt neither."

Desmond claimed to know where Luther Dubois lived. He told me he guessed he ought to since he'd been standing in Luther's front room when Luther stabbed him with a hunting knife.

"A repo way down here?" I asked him.

And Desmond told me, "Naw," but he didn't offer to explain exactly what he'd been about, so I waited on him to decide he'd probably have to.

"Getting something for Momma," he told me at last.

We then passed a minute in silence watching a boy flattening boxes behind the Kroger. He jumped up and down while smoking a butt and drinking a 7UP. He wasn't terribly thorough or noticeably industrious.

"She needs medicine sometimes," Desmond said. "Momma's got regular pain."

"Oh," I told him, and tried to make it sound tossed off and inconsequential, but in my mind I was laying that crooked wig to Oxy or Percocet.

"He cut you over money?" I asked him.

Desmond shook his head. "Just stabbed me."

"Why?"

"Can't really say. New knife maybe."

Desmond was folding and assembling his Sonic trash by then. By habit, Desmond bundled his wrappers and napkins and various spent condiment packets in a helpless display of anal compulsion that would have made NASA proud.

"Probably wanted to try it out."

I marked this down as another life-in-the-Delta lesson where a man might plunge a knife in a fellow just to see if he could.

"What did you do?" I asked Desmond.

"Bled all over everywhere. Luther drove me to the clinic. I'll give him that."

"How did you leave it with him?"

"I think I swore I'd kill him."

I pointed toward the floorboard as a means of asking Desmond if he meant to kill him now, today.

Desmond shook his head. "Might scuff him up a little, if that's all right."

We were soon back on the main artery into Yazoo City. It was pushing four o'clock as we headed toward downtown proper, which was two miles out a crapped-up four-lane where you couldn't get much worth having—discount shoes and mufflers, live bait and day-old bread.

The town itself was a lot less junky, but it didn't appear to be catching on. Downtown Yazoo was Greenville on a more modest scale.

The lampposts were baroque and limply hung with crimson YAZOO!! banners. The brick crosswalks had been laid in a herringbone pattern, and there were signs and awnings left from boutiquey stores that had opened and closed. About all you could get downtown was a haircut or a parking ticket.

In the spirit of revitalization, several roads had been rerouted into roundabouts that nobody seemed to know how to navigate. Right-of-way in downtown Yazoo City was speculative at best, and the planners had made the very most out of light to moderate traffic by confusing everybody to a crawl.

Desmond's steering style worked well for us. He sort of knew where he was going, but that hardly prevented our Geo from drifting all over the place, and Yazooites seemed to find it prudent to ease to the curb and let us pass.

Desmond hadn't been to Yazoo City in a pretty considerable while, so we toured the commercial desolation while he got his bearings. A couple of landmarks he had counted on had been torn entirely down, and one of them—an old rail depot—had been dressed up and transformed into a buffet restaurant in Ye Olde Bavarian style.

It had failed, of course, and the train platform had been heaped and piled with fencing to the extent that all we could see of the place was its Black Forest chalet roof. Desmond needed three passes to decide there was a depot underneath.

Neither one of us said a thing at all about the wretched state of the town, which was a sign to me that I was truly becoming acclimated. The Yazoo City we'd found was essentially the one we'd both expected.

Once Desmond had identified the depot, he knew where he wanted to go, and we finally left a roundabout for the road that he'd been after. It took us down by an old ice house, a couple of storefront churches, and then along a creek and into the countryside.

Quite suddenly, there weren't any buildings to speak of, mostly pines and scrub and kudzu, and once we'd passed the sheet-metal government warehouse where folks picked up their butter and cheese, we came to a couple of muddy feedlots packed with filthy cattle. Then we rolled up on the shabbiest housing development I'd ever seen.

The sign announcing the place on the road going in was no longer properly standing. CREEKSIDE ESTATES had been written on a square of plywood in spray paint. The signposts had rotted through and the whole thing had toppled over, but some industrious resident had propped it up with what was left of a lawn chair frame.

The creek in question was a ditch by the state road. The water in it was stagnant and standing.

The avenue into Creekside Estates was asphalt for about twenty yards, and where the county's obligation ended, the pocked and potted dirt road began. Desmond's straying hardly mattered since the surface was just a patchwork of craters, the deeper ones full of oily iridescent liquid, the sort that might have drained from a garbage truck.

There was stuff all along the margins of the road, some of it merely litter, but clothes as well and busted toys, furniture and plumbing fixtures, old microwaves, electric ranges, recliners and settees. It was hard to say if people had thought better of the crap they were hauling home or if that stretch of rough road was where they all decided they were close enough to the dump.

While Desmond looked for Luther's house, I scanned for the Ranchero. Aside from the color, it probably wouldn't have stood out all that much. The automobiles about were fine, probably worth more than the houses given that the predominant local roof treatment was royal blue plastic tarp. What money there was went for spinners and chrome running boards and Turtle Wax.

The roads were all named for Confederate generals, and Desmond recalled that Luther's house was at the end of Longstreet Street. We had to stop at about every corner to find out where we were because most of the signs had been knocked over or pulled down.

"We got a plan?" I asked.

"Planning on throwing Luther around a little."

"Won't Luther have a gun or something? A knife he wants to break in?"

"We're ready for him," Desmond told me, and gave my fireplace shovel a glance.

I wasn't quite prepared to think a fireplace shovel a plan.

"There it is." Desmond eased to a stop.

It was a rickety dump of a place with plastic on the windows and shutters on the ground. There was a kid on the porch. He looked four or five, too old for the diaper he was wearing and far too human for the nasty T-shirt he had on.

He also appeared more than a little Mexican to me, so I asked Desmond, "You sure this is Luther's place?"

He merely touched his scar and nodded.

We walked up and knocked. Desmond tried to convince me the child belonged to some customer of Luther's, but it turned out he was the son of the woman who answered the door.

Desmond asked her where Luther was, and she mounted an elaborate response, all of it rapid-fire and almost none of it in English. Except for *nope* and *meester,* she'd yet to pick up the local parlance.

"*Donde* Luther?" he asked this time around, and that woman told us all of it again.

She then advised her son, in a passionate aside, that he'd roast in hades if he kept picking his nose. It was conveyed in a blend of dumbshow and wishful theology. Beyond that, I couldn't decipher much of anything she said.

"I guess he moved," I told Desmond, who preferred that option to his nagging fear Luther was dead, which meant Desmond would never know the chance to kill him.

A neighbor across the road had come out by then to give us both the eyeball, and he cleared a few things up for us on several fronts at once.

He let us know niggers weren't welcome in Creekside Estates except, of course, for "yard work and shit." Then he told us he'd never so much as heard of a Luther Dubois and didn't know a thing about him bugging out because of the goddamn state police.

"Here's an idea," I said to Desmond. "Scuff *him* up instead." And Desmond was suddenly all sunshine and puppies.

That neighbor became a Constitutional scholar once we'd stepped into his yard. He was giving full voice to a rights and privileges catechism when Desmond supplied us all with a lesson in creative scuffing up. Desmond helped that gentleman visit far-flung precincts of his property through a combination of punching and tossing with a little stomping for garnish.

Desmond's style was uniquely his own, a kind of grappling with a difference, and that neighbor might as well have been Shawnica for all the effect he had on Desmond. He landed a blow or two up around Desmond's shoulders, but Desmond didn't appear to care. He'd just grab that neighbor by whatever was handy and launch him across the yard.

Some buddy of the neighbor's came rolling up the street and leapt out of his Camaro to help him. He took a run at Desmond, but went bouncing off and got set down pretty quick. He then came limping over my way to catch his breath and showed me the gun in his back pocket, a puny .22 automatic that might have held five rounds.

He made me to understand that since Desmond was black and not doing yard work and shit, he was probably the sort of nigger that needed shooting. I got to hear this from him, of course, because I was standing there being white.

My time in police departments all over the mid-South had

taught me two keystone principles I'd embraced and carried with me: Never tangle with an irate teenage girl if you can help it at all; and thumbs might be opposable, but they weren't meant to get bent back.

It was this second one I made use of on the gentleman with the pistol. I got a grip on his thumb and subdued him with a blend of torque and leverage. And by subdued, I mean he acted like I'd jerked his skeleton out.

He collapsed to the ground, whined and whimpered as I took his gun. Then he told me which shoe his money was in case I wanted that, too.

Across the street at Luther's old house, that toddler had shed his diaper and was having himself a rather majestic dump on his front walk. He watched Desmond while he picked his nose and got perused by a gangly hound that had come out from under the porch to see who exactly was using his toilet.

"You seeing this?" I asked Desmond.

Desmond eyed the toddler and nodded. "Maybe Dale's onto something after all."

Again my cracker offered up the money in his shoe. "There's not enough cash in the whole damn county," I told him, "to make me touch anything that's been next to your feet."

Then I twisted his thumb in a spirited, recreational sort of way and asked him, "Where did Luther Dubois get off to?"

"Tootie's," he told me, and said it straightaway. "Works out of there. Got anything you want."

I let him go, and he curled up whimpering on the ground like one of those children who pouts and mopes as opposed to the sort who flings off his diaper and shits on his own sidewalk.

I released the clip from that fellow's pistol and threw it over the house. I flung the gun itself into a kudzu patch at the end of Longstreet Street.

"Hey," I said to Desmond, "you know a place called Tootie's?"

Desmond nodded as "Satin Soul" struck up in his pocket. He fished his cell phone out. "You again," he told me, and tossed the phone my way.

Then he went back to scuffing up the neighbor, who, truth be told, was already about as scuffed as he needed to get.

"I thought I was supposed to call you," I said by way of hello.

"Wrinkle," Percy Dwayne told me. "Make it about twelve thirty."

"I haven't decided if I'm going to make it at all."

Then Percy Dwayne got earnest. You can always tell when a cracker has gone all grim and sincere because they start by way of preamble with some version of "Listen, buddy" and say it almost like an intimate whisper to make you pay attention.

My Dubois's choice was "Hey here, sport," and I fell silent as a courtesy while he told me everything I'd do and why.

Five thousand in twenties in a sack on the front porch of

some shit hole up in Webb, where they tend to specialize in shit holes. I doubted money in a sack on a porch up there would linger for very long.

Percy Dwayne was still a lot less particular about what I'd get in return. Gil's Ranchero. Somewhere. Sometime or another.

"All right," I told him. "Around twelve thirty."

"You're doing it then?" he asked me.

"I guess. You've got me by the short and curlies, don't you?"

"Damn straight," Percy Dwayne told me.

"I'll get to the bank in the morning. Half past twelve in Webb."

Percy Dwayne hooted with cracker delight. He dropped the connection hard like he'd bounced my Motorola off a wall.

Desmond tossed his fellow my way. He landed cringing at my feet. He looked a lot like I'd looked a little earlier in the day.

Desmond got us lost briefly in the bowels of Creekside Estates. We got turned around coming off Longstreet Street, took bad turns at Stuart and Hooker, and ended up on Lee Boulevard, the grand drag of the place.

I was reminded of Richmond's Monument Avenue. That appeared to be the model, anyway, but instead of statues of Confederate luminaries on horseback, Creekside Estates had live oaks down the middle of the road, and about every other one was rigged with a block and tackle and had a car engine dangling from it.

"Like Christmas," Desmond said.

"Or end times," I suggested.

SIX

Tootie's was about what you'd expect a Tootie's to be, particularly out in the countryside in Mississippi. It was an unpainted cinder-block roadhouse with—at only a little past six—a parking lot full of muddy pickup trucks.

There was no sign I could see, which caused me to ask Desmond, "You sure this is the place?"

"Oh yeah. Tootie'll be sitting at the end of the bar drinking an Iron City and smoking one of those stinking cherry cigars."

"Think Luther's in there?"

Desmond shrugged.

"How are we going to do this?"

"No *we* to it. You're going to do it. I'm too black to go in Tootie's. Not much chance I'd come out of there alive."

"Really?"

Desmond nodded. Desmond told me, "Cracker squared."

"What'll they do to me?"

"Sell you a beer for four dollars and, if Luther's around, about anything else you might need."

"What do I need?"

"Get some Oxy. Dicker with him. Luther loves that."

Desmond parked about as far away as he could get and still be on the property, well over where the lot ended and a weedy patch of stray junked cars began.

I've never been one of those guys who moves with ease through the human stratosphere, don't have a knack for talking to a farmer like a farmer or a mechanic like a mechanic. It doesn't matter who I get thrown in with, I'm always just my middling self. Sometimes that'll do, but every now and then it won't.

I could tell by the hooting and the shouting before I ever reached the door that Tootie's was full of lubricated Mississippi rednecks, and the worst thing I could do was try to pass as one of them. I decided, like usual, to be just me, only with a better story.

I doubt people smoke anywhere like people smoke in the South. And it's not the volume so much as the hunger they go at their cigarettes with, smoking each one like they'll never have another. Tootie's was full of people like that, men primarily along with a couple of creatures passing for women.

One of them was as big as Desmond, with hair so thin she

almost looked bald. The other was as bony as a refugee and hatchet-faced to boot.

It didn't matter. The men were lined up several deep to two-step with them, and the place was so blue with cigarette smoke that they all looked like they were dancing at the bottom of the sea.

Tootie's had a jukebox that played country crap of the Eddie Rabbit variety. A pool table with the felt in tatters. Some kind of dinging arcade game. The bar was a jackleg production made out of whatever had come to hand, and sure enough a fellow who had to be Tootie was parked at the far end. By bulk, he was probably carrying thirty pounds of neck and jowls.

He fixed on me once I'd stepped fully inside. They all did at least in passing, but Tootie was concentrated and altogether keen about it. Desmond had pegged him. He was drinking an Iron City straight out of the bottle and smoking a Swisher. I could smell it by the door.

The bartender, but for his extraordinary gut, looked remarkably like Popeye. He had a blond pompadour and a deficiency of teeth that made his chin jut out. He was inked, of course. Everybody's inked anymore from schoolgirls to navy admirals, but for some reason crackers seem disinclined to buy their tattoos retail.

On one forearm this guy had the face of a woman named Rita who looked a little like Thomas Jefferson but maybe half as pretty, and on the other he had what I guessed was an alligator, though it could have been a collie with scales.

I took a spot at the bar and waited for him to ask me what I wanted, and he finally did after a fashion. He glared at me, anyway, and said, "What?"

"Iron City if you've got it."

He huffed and slouched, acted like I'd asked him to paint my house.

"Four dollars," he said, and smacked the bottle down so hard before me that foam boiled out of the neck and beer pooled all over the place.

I drank the first one in silence, sat there looking closed off and morose, which was hardly much of a stretch with an Iron City to polish off. I had to wonder if Tootie had ever tasted an actual potable beer or had just gone through his jowly life drinking this skunky Pittsburgh lager.

The guy who'd last been dancing with the fat, bald woman came lurching up to the bar. His dungarees were greasy and his shirt was half-unbuttoned. He dug around in his pockets and came up with about eighty cents in change. He spilled it out on the bar top and ordered a Budweiser.

The bartender glanced at Tootie, who moved his head from side to side.

"Nope," Popeye said, and that customer snorted and growled like a mucousy bear.

Every time he moved, his stink hit me. It was a blend of body funk and dank earth with a hint of tractor diesel.

"Hey," he said, and I didn't need to see him to know he was talking to me. I showed Popeye my empty Iron City bottle by way of ordering another.

"HEY!" There was a useful touch of menace to it now.

I swung my head around to take him in. "What?"

"Buy me a cold one." He was thick-tongued and his eyes were wandering. He was missing most of his left ear. From the shape of what remained, it looked like somebody had gnawed it off.

He watched me, in as much as he could focus on anything, and drifted a little like he was fighting a wind.

Popeye slammed my Iron City down, and I closed my lips around the neck to soak up the nasty foam.

"HEY!"

This time I didn't even bother to glance.

"Buy me a damn beer," he said.

Most of the other patrons had taken an interest by now, including the bony, hatchet-faced girl who was plainly hoping for a brawl.

The dancing had stopped. The carousing had ebbed a little, and everybody in Tootie's was waiting to find out how pliable I might be. As they saw it, if things went their way, I could be setting up rounds all night. They'd just have to bore in with their bonhomie grins and threaten me a little.

So I had the audience I wanted and a fellow I thought I could manage by tapping him with a bar stool if it went as far as that.

Once I could feel him leaning my way and drawing breath to speak, I squared my shoulders to him and said, "Fuck off."

Then I shot him a quick, knuckly jab to the throat like I'd been taught at the academy. That boy sputtered and wheezed, coughed and stumbled. He was suddenly having so much trouble simply drawing breath that he could only manage to lean on the bar while he gurgled and stank.

I didn't say a thing to him, didn't really need to. Everybody in the place was watching him, but I just went back to my beer.

It was Desmond's full Shawnica treatment repurposed for drunken cracker louts.

He recovered after a few minutes and somebody else bought him a beer. I made a point of not really giving a happy shit who.

The whole business got Popeye's attention. He parked himself in front of me and asked me, "Do I know you?"

I thought he might ask me about my cuts and bruises, but he was kind of scuffed up himself. It seemed to be a state of nature with a class of people in the Delta.

I shook my head and told him, "Passing through," and I went all glum and heavy hearted and spilled out a story that would have made Merle Haggard proud.

I told him I was driving down from Wheeling, had come out of the mine to go fetch Momma in Houston, where they'd said they couldn't do a thing else with her at the cancer ward.

"She wants to be home with her people when she goes. Got a spot for her next to Daddy." Then I polished off my Iron City backwash, which helped with the wincing quite a lot.

Popeye, as it turned out, had a dead momma, and he got all misty about her. We trafficked between us in momma-centric platitudes for a time until I found an agreeable spot to complain about my back. It was damaged from the coal seam, but the drive down wasn't helping, and I'd gone and left my pain pills on the dresser at the house.

I let it go at that, didn't want to push it with Popeye. I shifted onto the goddamn federal government and all their goddamn shit.

It turned out I'd done enough. Popeye wandered down the bar and said a thing close and private to Tootie. He glanced at me and saw that I was a fool for Iron City just like him.

Tootie turned his jowly head and fairly barked out, "Luther."

Popeye came back to tell me, "This boy here'll help you out."

Luther Dubois materialized out of a gloomy back corner of the bar room. He was definitively seedy. Wiry and hard. Shifty and pestilential. He had about three days of growth on his chin but stank of aftershave.

I don't think I'd ever seen Sansabelt pants on a man so flabless and skinny. His polo shirt was linty and aquamarine. He was wearing cowboy boots with silver toe caps and rococo needlework on what looked to be fake-lizard hide. He was dressed like the sort of fellow you might come across on the public links in a circle of hell, or maybe Oklahoma.

"What you hunting?" Luther asked me, and grinned. The plaque on his teeth was so uninterrupted, it looked a little like piping.

I told him about my back. My momma. The ride down from Wheeling. Luther said he might have just the thing.

He invited me into his office. He said it with all the relish of a '70s TV hoodlum, and I followed him to a table back by the toilet door. For décor, Luther had a couple of Rolling Rock bottles and an overflowing ashtray.

"Oxy or Perk?" he asked me.

I shrugged. "Oxy, I guess."

"Codone or Contin?"

"I don't much care. Just need something to get me to Texas and back."

Luther stepped into the bathroom. He came out with a little plastic bag of tablets in is hand. "Buck and a half a milligram. I've got forties and eighties."

I'd been around the stuff enough up in Virginia to know Luther's was a bullshit price. You'd pay a dollar and a half a milligram if you were buying OxyContin at Le Cirque. An even dollar was on the high end of the going urban rate. In the uplands, depending on supply and factoring in desperation, a forty-milligram tablet of Oxy usually went for about thirty bucks.

"Seems high," I said.

Luther gave me a shrug, but I just stayed right where I was and waited. He lit a cigarette, a generic one that smelled like smoldering leaf litter, and took a leisurely pull on his Rolling Rock.

"For a friend of Tootie's I can maybe go one and a quarter."

"I'll give you sixty cents a mil," I said, and Luther had a bit of a cackling fit.

He got up and stalked around in a display of amused exasperation. This was drug dealing as opera for yokels.

"Sixty!? Shit! You hear that, Tootie?"

I think Tootie told him, "Uh-huh." I couldn't make him out over the music, but I saw a distinct jiggle in the folds in the back of his neck.

"A dollar ten," Luther countered. "You buy three eighties, I'll go an even buck."

"Take a check?"

Luther went on another prance around the roadhouse. He was laughing and hooting, but I could tell he was mostly showing off his boots. Luther would stop every now and again and buff the tops of them on his pant legs.

For a guy peddling pharmaceuticals out of the back of a bar, Luther didn't practice terribly much discretion. He yelled a fresh price at me from thirty feet away. You'd have thought we were transacting cattle on the hoof.

"Two forties at seventy cents," I told him. "That's all I've got to spend."

From the way Luther squinted, I could see he was trying to do some powerful calculating in his head.

"All right, then," he told me at last. "Forty-eight even. Cash money."

That must have qualified as higher math for a Delta cracker since he was off by a full eight dollars.

I dug around in my pockets. I didn't have forty-eight. I

needed dimes and nickels to even make forty-five. I showed it to Luther, and he looked like he might go on a circuit again, but it turned out he was one of those people weak in the face of legal tender.

I had cash in my hand. I was offering it to him, and he couldn't help but take it. It didn't matter what he was asking. He was built to get what he got.

My two pills were a little grimy, which seemed to suit the circumstances. Popeye reached over the bar and shook my hand as I was leaving. It's a wonder sometimes what the love of even a fictional momma can do.

In my absence, Desmond had backed deeper into the weedy patch, and was hidden from view behind a junked dump truck. I panicked a little when I didn't see him at first. Then he blinked his headlights at me. Blinked, anyway, the one that still worked.

"He's in there," I told him, and showed Desmond my pair of pills.

He held his hand out, palm up, and had me drop them in it. "Momma's got pain," he said.

What was I going to tell him? "All right."

Desmond pointed out a greasy cable laid up on the Metro dash. "Coil wire," Desmond told me. "Took it off Luther's car."

"You knew he was in there?"

"Stood to reason."

"So this is kind of about Luther and kind of about Momma's pain?"

Desmond nodded. Desmond told me, "Kind of."

It grew dark as we sat there, and finally somebody came reeling out of Tootie's. It was the boy who'd demanded a beer. We watched him lurch across the lot, fling open the door of his pickup, and blunder under the wheel. It took him about a quarter hour to get the key in the ignition. He started the engine, revved it to screaming, and dropped the transmission into gear.

I was about to tell Desmond, "Uh-oh," when that boy roared out of the lot. He shot straight across the road and into a soybean field. He just kept going for as long as he could until the truck sank in and mired up to the axles.

He tried to rock loose, but his transmission seized and his engine stalled out dead. We could hear his radio a little. He blew his horn a couple of times and swore quite a lot. Then, instead of climbing out and walking back to Tootie's for help, he went (as best as we could tell) to sleep.

SEVEN

I was beginning to think Luther would never come out when Tootie's door finally swung open and cast a shaft of light in the lot that Luther came prancing into. He unzipped his pants and hosed off Tootie's front wall while simultaneously lighting a cigarette. Then he closed his trousers, polished his boot tops, and headed off to his car.

His was some variation on Desmond's vehicle. Puny. Boxy. Kind of a city junker in the middle of nowhere much. Aside from pickups and tricked-out Escalades, that's about all you'd ever see on the roads down here. They're cheap to own and cheap to run, almost disposable, really, so it's never terribly surprising when one of them won't start.

Luther's included. He cranked the engine for three or

four minutes. We could hear the squeak of the throttle as he pumped the gas. The thing just ground away and didn't threaten to catch.

We watched him climb out of his coupe and lift the hood. Luther surveyed the engine, not like a man who knew a thing about internal combustion but more like one who knew where the engine was. He poked around a little. He pulled something off and put it back on, jiggled a wire or two. Then he glanced around the parking lot, almost on the sly. Instead of looking for help, he appeared to be sizing up something to drive away.

"Why don't you give him a hand," Desmond suggested.

I'd have been suspicious to see me, but Luther didn't blink when I wandered over to ask him what his trouble might be. I'd left Tootie's two hours ahead of him and was still out in the lot.

"Catching some winks," I said by way of explanation, but Luther didn't care. I guess with his clientele, most any damn thing was normal.

"She won't go," he told me, and gave his car a theatrical sort of kick that showed his gaudy boots to best effect.

"Try it again," I said, and Luther climbed in and turned the engine over while, shielded by the hood, I stood there doing nothing to help him along. "How about now?" Luther turned the key again.

He'd just joined me at the front grille when Desmond came up out of nowhere. That was one of Desmond's leading skills. He was crafty and quiet and, once he slipped up on you, bigger than you could hope to do much of anything about.

Desmond eased up behind Luther, and Luther appeared to sense him. He got a look on his face like he was about to throw an aneurysm.

When he wheeled and saw Desmond, he said, "You told me to stick you! Remember?"

Desmond clapped his hands together with Luther's head between his palms, and Luther went entirely senseless straightaway.

"You told him to stick you?"

Desmond ignored me. "Get his feet," he said.

We carried Luther toward Desmond's car, but I couldn't figure what we were up to.

"Where are we going to put him?" I asked Desmond.

"In the back," he said.

"What back?"

Come to find out, you can get a grown man in the back of a Metro. He just has to be unconscious so you can bend him and stuff him behind the passenger seat.

"We'll take him somewhere and chat him up," Desmond offered as a plan.

We'd forced Luther into the way back by shoving him down headfirst, which left his legs and feet sticking up in the air. So his gaudy boots were handy for Desmond to pull off.

He wedged one in front of each rear tire and ran over them a couple of times before we pulled out of Tootie's lot and chugged off into the Mississippi night.

We had regrets on the road, of course, due to the stink of Luther's feet.

We pulled in for gas at a Qwik Stop near Belzoni. I was standing at the pump island putting in ten dollars exactly for Desmond when a fellow pulled up on the other side to fill his muddy Ranger.

He saw Luther's feet in the way back, laughed, and asked, "Who the fuck's that?"

I didn't have Desmond to supply me with the proper Delta answer. He'd gone into the shop for a hunk of monkey bread. It was the only food that would sustain him when a Coney Island wasn't at hand.

In most places I would have just said Luther was drunk and had a laugh with that fellow at the gas pump, but nobody in the Delta ever let alcohol keep them from fighting or driving. You could be a Primitive Baptist—a sober subset of the place—or you could be a passably functioning alcoholic. You couldn't be just passed out and shoved in the back of a Metro. That would qualify as suspicious in the Delta.

"His wife caught him with her sister. She like to beat him to death." I reached in through the passenger window and pulled out my fireplace shovel, showed it to that fellow at the pump island as a narrative visual aid.

It turned out he'd had a thing with an in-law once and had gotten in a row about it. He took off his cap, parted his hair, and showed me a scar on the top of his head.

"Get it worked out?" I asked him.

"Had three babies since then."

The average Delta romance—excluding the girls from the cotillion in Greenville—was less candlelight and champagne than antibiotics and midnight sutures.

Desmond came out with his mouth full as that fellow pulled away, and I suggested we might want to extract Luther and chat him up sooner than later.

Desmond agreed to the extent that he drove north another dozen miles or so before he turned off on a side road and pulled in behind a church. It was one of those frame black churches of the Temple-Mount-Nazarene-Zion-of-the-Lamb variety with a string of letters after the name like it had gone to dental school.

It had a cemetery with the graves sunk in and the markers tilted and pitched from the heaving ground. We parked around by the propane tank where there was a vapor light, hauled Luther out, and laid him on the hood. It turned out he'd been awake for a pretty good while, just pinned tight by the seat back and resting.

When he opened his mouth, he started in just where he'd left off. "Because I wouldn't have stuck you unless you told me to."

I had to reach in and stop Desmond from clapping Luther's head between his hands again.

"Why would he tell you to stab him?" I asked Luther.

"He was all fucked up back then. Ask him."

So I did. "Shawnica?"

Desmond and Luther nodded in unison.

Luther then asked us both together, "Where'd my boots get to?"

Desmond pointed south into the Mississippi night.

Luther looked tempted to set up an ugly fuss about his boots until Desmond rang his bell with a lone open hand to reprioritize him.

"A cousin of yours stole his car," Desmond said. "You're going to help us get it back."

"What cousin?"

"Percy Dwayne."

Luther groaned. "First place," he told us, "he's my uncle, not my cousin. Second, I can't do nothing with him."

"He's a good ten years younger than you," I said. "How's he your uncle?"

Desmond and Luther looked at me like I'd asked them where mud comes from. I hadn't thought it through, of course. There's a whole class of people in the Delta who have strings of children the way Calcutta swells have polo ponies. I'd seen more than a few grandmotherly Dubois sorts with babies on their hips that they sure weren't treating like grandchildren. A toddler could easily be an uncle to a grown man in these parts.

"How did he come to have your car?" Luther asked me.

I lifted my head so the vapor light showed off my cuts and my contusions.

"Oh," Luther said. "I just figured some fellow beat you up."

"Some fellow did," I told him.

And Luther had a Kendell moment. "Percy Dwayne!?" he said, and stuck out a hand at gay, dwarf hanger-on height.

"Came up behind me with a shovel."

I tried not to sound all whiny and defensive, but then Luther snorted and treated me to a sneer, so I clapped his head between my hands once hard.

I lack Desmond's natural force and bulk and so failed to knock Luther out cold, but I rocked him enough to make him whimper a little.

"What the hell you need me for?" Luther wanted to know. "If you know what he took and know who took it, why don't you call the law?"

Me and Desmond glanced at each other, lost for an explanation we'd be willing to share with Luther, but he provided us in the interval a workable one of his own. "Car stole before he stole it?" he asked us.

That seemed handy enough, so we nodded and told him, "Yep."

"We might work something out," Luther said in his come-into-my-office sort of way.

"It's worked out," Desmond told him. "You're going to help us find him, and we're going to make you wish you had every time you don't."

"I'll need my boots."

"They're back at Tootie's," I told him. "We'll get you something else."

We let him ride upright this time or as upright as he could get in what passes in a Metro for a back seat.

What we learned on the way up 49 was that Luther couldn't shut up. He told us every little thing he remembered about his uncle Percy Dwayne, most of it inflammatory and incriminating. Some of it so glancing and inconsequential that Luther would forget what he was going on about before he was halfway through.

Then Luther treated us to the ghastly intimate details of a fling he'd lately had with the fat, bald woman from Tootie's. Though she looked like a Fred or a Dewey, her name was Tiffany, as it turned out. Luther described what they'd gotten up to with the arid precision of an electrical engineer detailing a wiring chart.

"Shut it!" I told him at last.

"You boys ain't no fun," Luther said. "Him particular." He pointed at Desmond. "Went all straight and shit, didn't you?"

Desmond made the sort of necknoise you might hear from a Kodiak bear if you got close enough to be eaten by one for dinner.

"Hey," Luther said, and poked the back of Desmond's shoulder. "Bet Momma ain't on the high road with you."

"Hit him," Desmond told me. I was inclined that way already.

I had just enough room to work my arm like a piston, and I caught Luther flush between the eyes. His head bounced off the rear window glass, and Luther napped for a bit.

We were up near the crossroads at the truck route, and we both seemed to know where we were heading without having discussed it at all.

"What if Dale's there?" I asked.

"We'll send him in first," Desmond told me. Luther was just beginning to stir by then. "Can't ride around all night."

With that, Desmond cut west in the direction of Indianola, took some back road by Centralia, and came up from the south, just in case Dale had some buddies laying for us on the truck route.

We rolled by Pearl's a couple of times. It was a little past nine by then. She had lights she rarely switched on burning all over the house.

"Why's that?" Desmond asked, but I couldn't truly say, so we decided that was the sort of thing Luther could find out for us, Luther who claimed to be awfully goddamn tired of finding himself knocked out.

"Fair enough," I told him. "You do for us, and we'll stop beating on you."

"I'll be needing a little folding money as well."

"Let's see how it goes," I said. "You help us with Percy Dwayne, help us get my car back, and I'll try to make you whole."

We stopped at the head of Pearl's block, and I pointed Pearl's house out to Luther.

"There's a car shed in the back. Apartment up top. Go unlock it and turn the lights on. Then look around and see if anybody's about." I pulled the key off my ring and gave it to him.

"Who are you expecting?" Luther asked me.

I shrugged. "Nobody really."

"And if it's somebody, what do I tell him?"

"Tell him you're feeding the cat."

"What's the cat's name?"

"Isn't a cat."

Luther got all over me for not observing his primary rule of espionage: Only lie when you have to.

"I'm going to tell him I'm watering your plants instead." Then he tapped his temple with his finger as a sign of how shrewd he was.

I let him out of the Geo and stood there looking out over the roof as Luther walked up the street in his socks and turned into Pearl's driveway.

"Got any plants?" Desmond asked me.

"No," I said.

Desmond kept the motor running and the car in gear, and I climbed back in so we'd be ready to go. I think we half expected to see Dale or one of his musclehead cracker colleagues come charging out of Pearl's house armed like SWAT and firing grenades and such. But nothing happened and nothing continued to happen for longer than we'd hoped.

Then we got uneasy and feared that Luther might be ransacking the place or going cross-country out to the truck stop in hopes of flagging down a cruiser. Luther was just one to figure there'd be some reward for him in turning us in.

So we climbed out of the Geo and hovered by it for a time.

"What do you think?" Desmond kept asking me, and I

kept not exactly knowing, until Luther finally strolled down the driveway. We could hear the click of his shoes, and he looked to be wearing a seersucker sports coat as well.

"Looks to me," I said to Desmond, "Luther got insisted at."

"Pearl's looking for you," Luther told me. Then he opened his jacket to show us the sateen lining. "Just like new."

The shoes were fine black leather oxfords, though a little wingtippy and tooled half to death, but that was just in Luther's line. Better still they had taps on the heels.

"It seems that husband of hers," he told us, "used to be quite the dancer." Luther wheeled around so we could better take him in.

"Come on," he told us. "Pearl's got supper waiting."

EIGHT

Pearl, as it turned out, was in insisting heaven. Luther was naturally primed to steal everything she had, and Pearl was possessed of a burning need to hand all of it over. So they were enjoying a natural sync you don't usually find with humans. The two of them were cackling over some private joke on the steps of Pearl's back porch by the time me and Desmond had made it up the drive.

Desmond had been by a time or two before, and Pearl had visited some fudge on him that had turned out to be a little blue and fuzzy in the middle, so Desmond was a lot more guarded than Luther about getting insisted at.

I was a little done in, and I was trying to figure some way

out of supper until a woman came out of Pearl's house and joined Pearl on the steps.

She was lovely and stylish, tall and fit. She looked out of place in the Delta. I was afraid for a moment she'd open her mouth and spoil it all with her chatter, but she didn't talk like one of those syrupy Delta princesses who seem intent on saying nothing without end and all the time. She was pleasant and warm and seemed happy to meet us, which is more than I would have been if I'd been her and we'd rolled up with Luther in the dark.

She was Pearl's only sister's child, Angela Marie, who Pearl talked about so much I'd long since tuned her out. I knew she worked in a Memphis hospital, and I'd just figured she was a nurse and had pictured a homely, dumpy girl wandering the wards in her whites. It turned out, though, she ran the place, and she insisted we call her Angie.

"My," she said once she'd seen my welts and bruises in the porch light.

"Wrong end of a shovel," I told her.

"Why don't you come in here."

She sat me down in Pearl's kitchen under Pearl's green-tinged fluorescents, which had the effect of making us all look a little mortuarial. Me more than Angie, who kept looking lovely if only a little too wan.

She cupped my chin in her hand and tilted my face up where she could see it best.

"Are you a doctor?" I asked her.

"Never practiced," she said. "Anybody seen you yet?"

"No."

Angie sent Pearl off for peroxide and cotton. "Headache?" she asked me.

"Not anymore."

"Your nose is broken."

"I figured."

"I can probably straighten it up."

I was about to tell her not to bother when she reached up and jerked the cartilage back where it had started out the morning. I think I screamed like a teenage girl at a slumber party.

"There," she said, and took the bottle from Pearl so she could have the further pleasure of dashing peroxide on my wounds.

As meetings go, it wasn't terribly auspicious from my end, but Pearl's niece seemed to enjoy the chance to practice without a license, and it was a pleasant surprise to have an age-appropriate woman touch me for the first time in a while. Pearl had made supper enough for about a dozen people while Angie, I guess, had been roaming around turning all the lights on in the house.

The main entrée was a casserole. This one was capped with a layer of crumbled potato chips and alarmingly orange cheese. It took main force for Pearl to even pass a serving spoon through the crust. There was chicken and peas and carrots and milky gravy underneath.

Luther went into raptures. Now that he had his seersucker jacket on, he looked like he was ready for a night at the country club buffet.

It turned out Luther was truly slick with a compliment. Pearl would insist without encouragement, but Luther wasn't taking any chances and handed out high purple kudos on every damn thing he could think of. The casserole itself. The place settings. The napkin rings. The glorious drop-leaf table. The sachet in the bowl on the sideboard. The silk ivy centerpiece. He went down the list of everything he could call by name and congratulated Pearl on having had the sterling taste to buy it.

It was a little hard for me to reconcile the Luther at Pearl's with the one I'd met at Tootie's, and I was half tempted to reconsider my low opinion of him until I saw Luther slip a fork into his pocket.

"So you're the Nick Reid I've been hearing so much about," Angie said. "Pearl tells me you're in electronics."

"Mostly," I told her. "Me and Desmond work together. We're sort of into anything people stop payment on. Probably electronics primarily these days."

"And you used to be a policeman?" she asked me, which came as an appreciable shock to Luther, whose interest in Pearl's décor quite suddenly drained away.

I nodded. "Up in Virginia."

"That must have been interesting."

"Wears on you after a while. You don't see people at their best."

Luther handed Pearl plates to help her serve and sang the praises of his jacket. He told her me and Desmond had been quick to admire his shoes. That delighted Pearl, who never got awfully much feedback on her insisting. People usually took stuff from her to shut her up. Me, I mean. I don't think anybody else much bothered with her.

Pearl made us hold hands and say grace. I peeked around while we were in the middle of giving thanks. It was the oddest sort of dinner party I ever hope to attend and got stranger once Angie had begun to quiz Luther on the details of his career.

Luther claimed to be an entrepreneur, a facilitator, and gadget mogul. Luther, it seems, had invented a pecan cracker that worked with a carriage bolt and a rubber band.

I've got to hand it to him, Luther could just about pass for decent and proper and seemly. He gave the impression of being civilized there at the dining table until he pulled out his pack of generic cigarettes and shook one out for Pearl.

"Take it outside," I told him, and he looked at me stricken and shocked that there could be a place where a fellow couldn't light up at the table and then crush his butt out on the dab of casserole he'd left.

"Out," I said.

Luther decided instead he'd be better off helping Pearl clear.

Pearl and Luther eventually went back to pilfering through Gil's wardrobe while me and Desmond and Angie stayed at the table and drank weak coffee.

"Did Pearl tell you about Gil's car?" I asked.

"What car?"

We all walked outside to the car shed, and I opened the doors on the empty bay. Angie looked a little shocked to see the state of it. Not that it was empty but that it was tidy and all but antiseptic.

"Wow," she said. "I don't guess Pearl was ever in here."

"Gil had a Ranchero," I told her. That was news to Angie. "Must have been his baby. It was all buttoned up in here."

"Where'd it go?"

I told her the whole story. I didn't polish it up, and I just laid it out like it happened, even the parts that made me look foolish and irredeemably rash.

The nut of it was that I'd made a binding pledge to Pearl to bring Gil's Ranchero back just like I'd driven it away, and I explained to Angie how it didn't matter if Pearl wanted it back or not and if it ever left the car shed bay again. The point was I'd sworn an oath, and I intended to fulfill it.

Angie turned to Desmond and asked him, "Is he always like this?"

Desmond nodded, told her, "Pretty much."

"Might take a few days," I told her.

"Okay," was all she said.

Just then Luther popped out of the house in a pair of Gil's immaculate coveralls, which he was wearing under a double-breasted suit coat. The shoes he had on now had taps on the toes as well as the heels.

"Gil tapped?" I asked Angie.

Angie shrugged. "Didn't know that, either."

Pearl followed Luther out. She looked about as pleased as I'd ever seen her. Luther's enthusiasm at getting something for nothing was serving as an elixir for Pearl. Of course I couldn't help but wonder how Gil was making out in the churchyard by now, if he was only rotating or had achieved full Mach 2 spin.

"Did you tell him about the officer?" Pearl asked her niece.

"The one you hit," Angie said to me. "Dale?"

I nodded.

"He came by a couple of hours ago looking for you."

"Just him?"

She nodded.

"How was he?"

"His head was all wrapped up. Otherwise, just big and dumb."

Luther had gotten busy putting on his own spontaneous fashion show. He was twirling around in the driveway, raising clatter with his taps. He kept inviting us to admire his suit coat and the way it draped and hung.

"Tell you the truth," Luther said while picking a speck of lint off of his sleeve, "I wouldn't ordinarily much like getting snatched and hauled up here. Where the hell are we, anyway?"

"Indianola," Pearl informed him.

"But I've got to say," Luther went on, "this thing is sort of working out."

NINE

I can't say I had a legitimate plan, but I did have an idea. Pearl dug up a couple of pairs of scissors, and I left Desmond and Luther in her kitchen cutting dollar-bill-sized sheets out of her accumulated newspapers. Luther had gotten into Gil's dress hats by then and was wearing a Dobbs fedora, the kind with the jaunty feather in the band that made the work seem festive and gay.

For my part, I conscripted Angie to drive me to the shopping plaza in her car, just in case Dale and his buddies were out there laying for the Geo. I had her park up between the dollar store and the KFC and wait for me while I walked down to K-Lo's and slipped up from the rear.

Everybody who worked for K-Lo knew how to get in the store without the responsibility and bother of a key. K-Lo had gone cheap on his back metal door, so if you knew just where to pry it, there was play enough to ease the bolt entirely from the keeper.

The thieves K-Lo was plagued with of late didn't bother with the back. They usually drove up on the sidewalk and rammed the front doors in.

I figured K-Lo would be drunk and out on the sales floor somewhere. I had a reasonable fear that K-Lo might have gotten his shotgun loaded before he went about the business of loading himself. That wouldn't have taken long because K-Lo couldn't hold his liquor. He drank almost every night. Always Armagnac and Coke in a Solo cup on ice, and he'd get stewed straightaway and all at once.

I thought maybe he was playing the radio at first, but it turned out he was singing, and he was doing a fairly remarkable imitation of der Bingle's "Swinging on a Star."

I was just about stunned, to be honest, because K-Lo didn't fraternize. We got to see him fight with his wife, but that was incidental. K-Lo didn't ever confide in us, wasn't the sort to tell us a thing. He was just the guy who gave us scraps of paper and sent us out into the Delta, railed at us with devastating surgical skill whenever we made him unhappy, paid us once every two weeks without fail, and stayed behind when we went home.

I only knew for certain that K-Lo loved a dollar and

refused to eat Chinese. I hadn't really imagined the man could sing.

My job was to take his shotgun before K-Lo noticed me. He was parked out on a settee, the one he couldn't sell or lease because it was uglier even than the worst sort of Delta trailer trash could stand for. It had skirting and tufts and buttons, and the fabric was hideous plaid, all married in a way to make for universal homeliness.

I came up slowly, silently, picked my way through the store, and the closer I drew to K-Lo, the better his Bing Crosby got. He had the croon and the burble down cold, and his timing was damn good, too, for a hotheaded Lebanese American living on a bayou in Leland.

"You could be better than you are."

He'd left his shotgun leaning on the sofa back, stock wedged behind a cushion and barrel to the ceiling.

I grabbed the barrel and drew the thing to me.

"You could be swinging on a . . . SHIT!"

K-Lo saw me, leapt to his feet, and went scrabbling for his gun, but he wasn't even looking where he'd left it, just scratching around any old where as he blistered me with abuse.

"Calm down," I said. "It's just me."

K-Lo studied me for a moment and then recalibrated so he could lace me for a solid minute with a personalized tirade. Ronnie the tattooed felon might have wept, but I'd already had a character-building day.

K-Lo dropped down hard on the ugly settee, and I circled

around and sat beside him. Neither one of us said anything for about a half a minute until I broke the ice with, "Mean Bing."

K-Lo nodded. "He had pipes."

"How's Dale?"

K-Lo shrugged. "Some stitches. He'll be okay."

"And Patty?"

K-Lo shook his head. "Pissed," was all he told me.

K-Lo took a draw on his Armangac and Coke. "Found my TV yet?"

I shook my head. "But we're on it."

Just then a ghetto-fabulous Mazda pulled into the shopping plaza. The aftermarket grille alone was worth more than an engine rebuild, and I could have spent two weeks in Cancún on the price of the free-spinning wheels. The driver turned off his headlights, and that coupe cruised through the lot.

The shopping plaza was empty. Half the storefronts were vacant due to ongoing Delta retail strife, and the ones that were still occupied had long since closed for the night. That Mazda rolled into a corner, deep in shadow, and everybody got out. Three at least. Maybe four. Over from Greenville, I figured, where the lowlives there had probably run out of places to rob.

K-Lo hadn't been hit in nearly three months. That was almost an unprecedented stretch.

"Come on," I told him. I led K-Lo back toward his office as I checked the shotgun load. K-Lo had slammed in six rounds of rubber buckshot—good for driving off bears or anarchists. I ejected one to look it over. RIOT READY, the casing read.

"When did you get these?"

"Week or so ago. I'd just as soon make them sorry as dead."

"Hmm," I said in just the way that Desmond would have said it. Riot Ready rubber buckshot felt to me at the moment like a means of high-velocity therapy.

I left K-Lo in his office and went out the back door. I circled around to the retail side of the place. There were three big, strapping black kids and one wiry older guy whose job apparently was to wonder why nobody was doing what he'd asked them to do. They had a wonder bar and a hacksaw. A come-along, a pair of bolt cutters.

K-Lo had long since sprung for a titanium plate on the door gap, so there wasn't anything to pry or saw, nothing to draw or cut. Those boys might as well have brought a sugar spoon.

The trouble was with the wiry guy. He loved his Mazda too much. The tried-and-true way into K-Lo's was to just drive through the front glass. Then you grabbed what you could, rolled your car out, and headed back to Greenville. Nobody ever got away with more than about a thousand dollars of goods, but they kept just making the same Godawful mess.

Me and Desmond had once tried to convince K-Lo to leave a TV on the sidewalk. A kind of thug offering to help to keep his plate glass in tact. K-Lo hadn't done it. He thought it wasn't manly. K-Lo was big on manliness. He was Mexican that way.

If I waited around for a crime scene, I feared I'd be there half the night since those fellows didn't have among them the tools or apparently the smarts they needed to get in. For my part, I had Riot Ready loads and some frustration to work off, so I decided I wouldn't wait for an actual crime. I decided this would be about me.

"Fellows," I said, and before any of them could draw out whatever thug-life pistols they were packing, I aimed that shotgun barrel just over their heads and squeezed off a load. Once they'd lit out for their Mazda coupe, I leveled that Beretta and fired again. I didn't want to blind them after all.

I was taking a lesson from Desmond. Rubber buckshot was just my way of scuffing those fellows up. From the fuss they raised, I could tell I was making capable work out of it.

I kept firing until they'd all piled in the car and left the lot. I could hear those rubber pellets zipping and bouncing all over the place.

It was purely exhilarating, and by the time they were out of range I was probably hearing about half as well as Dale. So I didn't know Angie was racing up until she'd pulled into the lot.

She'd heard the shots from over by the KFC and had driven right toward trouble instead of sitting or driving the other way. I knew if I owned an Acura and had a career, I'd be deaf to a lot of things. In particular gunfire at a deserted shopping plaza.

I screamed at her I was fine. We walked together around to the back door, where K-Lo met us with a ball-peen hammer. Aside from his shotgun, it was all he had to ward off burglars with.

I tried to introduce him to Angela Marie, but K-Lo was far too agitated for even marginal civil discourse, which left us to stand there in the stockroom and watch K-Lo be upset.

"They won't be back," I told him.

"More where they came from," K-Lo said.

He then retired to the sales floor to plop down on the homely plaid settee. We followed him. Angie insisted. This was her first exposure to K-Lo. I didn't see him sad and drunk too often. I was accustomed to irate.

He looked up at us. He was nearly in tears. "They took my cat," he said.

"His cat?" Angie asked me.

"Bobcat," I told her.

"He had a bobcat?"

"Stuffed."

K-Lo was weeping by now in a near-hysterical Middle Eastern sort of way.

"Somebody broke in three months ago and stole it. Meant a lot to him."

K-Lo had started in on a kind of ululation. It was part der Bingle and part, I guess, atavistic Lebanese.

"Let me ask you something," I said to K-Lo. "Did I just drive those fellows a ways?"

He nodded.

"Did I just keep them from breaking in here and busting your place all up?"

Another nod.

"Now don't you feel like you owe me a little something?"

K-Lo just looked at me. Owing wasn't really his game.

I bulled on ahead. "Here's what I need—three hundred dollars in twenties, and this shotgun for a day or two. Maybe all your Riot Ready shells."

K-Lo winced. He muttered to himself. After a great long while, he nodded. He left me and Angie on the sales floor while he went back to get the cash.

K-Lo gave me all the twenties he could scare up in the petty-cash lockbox. Not quite three hundred dollars, but close enough. The shotgun shells he just pointed me to. Then he plopped down heavily in his chair like he was weary and spent from having been all saintly.

"You need to go home," I told him, and he tried to wave me off until I promised him I'd call his wife to see what she had to say about it.

Me and Angie helped him to his Civic and got him situated behind the wheel. We pointed him right and sent him off like he was in the Soap Box Derby. He lurched up on the curbing as he left the shopping plaza.

"Will he make it?" Angie asked me.

"Always does," I said.

I locked up the store and circled around with Angie to her Acura in the lot.

"Hell of a gun," she told me along the way, and took the

thing out of my hands. "Don't see too many Berettas in these parts." It was clear from the way she handled it that she knew what she was about.

"You hunt?"

"Used to. Just ducks. Me and Uncle Gil."

"Don't know that I'd have figured him for a hunter. How many hobbies can one guy have?"

"It was more about me than him. He didn't like getting in the water. Didn't like sitting in the blind. Didn't want to shoot anything he'd have to pluck and gut."

"So what did he like?"

"A day with his niece."

We didn't say much beyond that until she'd pulled to the roadside in front of Pearl's and I apologized for all the tumult and thanked her for her help.

"This is fine with me," she said. "Pearl'd usually be making me go through her closet."

Luther was back into leisurewear at the kitchen table, not his circle-of-hell golfing ensemble but something else of Gil's he and Pearl had turned up. The slacks were pleated and peg-legged both, which made Luther look like some sort of mobster genie at play. His shirt was ivory knit with a gray and pinkish argyle vest on top.

"How's it going?" I asked generally.

To hear it from Luther and Pearl, things were going splendidly well.

Desmond, for his part, told me, "He ain't much help."

I fished the twenties K-Lo had given me out of my pockets and laid them on the table.

"You're not going to tell them what happened?" Angie asked.

"Had to drive off some boys trying to break in at K-Lo's."

Pearl made out to be aghast, but Luther and Desmond couldn't be bothered. Thievery had long since become as common in the Delta as blues tourists or biting flies.

We all went straight back to the business at hand. It didn't look at first like they'd cut enough paper to make the illusion work, but once we'd started stacking it up and making bundles from it, I was persuaded we could probably get by.

Pearl supplied us with rubber bands, some of them even unrotted, and we laid a twenty on top of each stack before we bound it tight. We ended up with eight piles of what looked, at first glance, to be uninterrupted money.

Luther launched into an explanation of how crackheads and Delta junkies and even his uncle that Dubois would think it was more cash than it was because they never saw money in actual piles.

We laid the stacks in a paper sack with all the twenties showing, and we took turns lifting it off the table and being satisfied.

"What's this for?" Pearl finally asked me.

I told her straight up that I'd be buying back Gil's Ranchero from that fellow who had beat me with his fireplace shovel and driven it off.

"When's this?" Luther wanted to know.

"Tomorrow. Around noon. Up in Webb," I told him.

"You need to go home?" I asked Desmond.

"I need to go home," Luther said.

"Nobody's talking to you." I told him. "We're not finished yet."

Desmond weighed his momma's pain against the chance of running into Dale. He finally told me, "Think I'll just stick here."

Even given the hour, Angela Marie was determined to drive back to Memphis. That was a three-hour trip no matter how you cut it.

"Watch yourself," I told her. "There are K-Lo's all over the place."

She handed me one of her business cards. "Let me know how this turns out."

"All right."

"Maybe one day we can go duck hunting."

"I can sit in a blind and drink about as well as anybody."

I didn't realize how small and cramped my car shed apartment was until me and Desmond and Luther were all inside it. It was a little better than sleeping in the Geo, but not that much. I offered my bed to Desmond, but he preferred the floor. Not the floor dressed up for sleeping and made to pass for some kind of palette, but just the floor as it was— uncarpeted wood.

Once Desmond got down on it, he lay on his back and went right to sleep.

I tend toward insomnia and couldn't help but resent him a little, all the more once Luther started to talk.

He was stretched out on the sofa. I was across the room in the bed. Luther seemed primed to chat at me for a while. He had nothing specific in mind, but he was still giddy from all the swell shit Pearl had insisted on him, and he went through the list and described each item in turn.

Then he told me there were fish that lived in trees. He said there was liquor made from cobras that he wouldn't fucking drink and a beer he'd had once at a bar in Jackson that was brewed in outer space. He said he was married one time for about a day and a half. Had a foot fungus two years back he'd cured with Clorox. He wondered what Muslims were up to in a general sort of way. Then he just stopped talking because he was asleep.

TEN

As for me, I didn't sleep at first. By *at first* I mean from midnight until about half past three. Desmond was snoring on the floor, and Luther was wheezing on the couch. He sounded like he was trying to bring up a hairball.

Worse still, Luther had insisted on stripping down to his underwear alone. He'd flung back his blanket and was all uncovered and revealed. His underwear was alarmingly brief, what passes in Walmart for man-sexy.

Luther, in keeping with the cracker tradition, was tatted up across his chest. He had a likeness of Dale Earnhardt over his left nipple and a flat-bottomed fishing boat just above his right. There was something coming up over his shoulder, either a dragon or Tammy Wynette. His midriff featured what appeared at first like a snatch of Latin in Gothic script. I got a closer look on the way to the toilet. It wasn't Latin after all but *Go Fuck Yourself* all done up and ornate.

I awoke gradually to crows having a spat in the neighboring live oak. The sun was well up, and the apartment was as fragrant as a stockyard. Desmond was still snoring, and I shifted around to find Luther alongside me in the bed. So I woke all the way up in an alarming hurry.

Luther stretched and groaned. "Sofa didn't cut it." Then he told me, "Watch this," arched his back, and broke loud, clammy wind.

I was on my feet so fast that I was dizzy.

As best I could tell, Desmond hadn't moved so much as an inch. He looked like a chalk outline waiting to happen.

"You in there?" I asked him.

Desmond gave me a grunt by way of reply but just stayed where he was, laid out on the floor. No cover. No pillow. No nothing.

"Not opening my eyes until Luther puts on his pants."

Luther's morning ritual seemed to consist entirely of vaporish behavior. When he wasn't making showy exhibitions of breaking wind, he was burping or preparing for a belch. I made him get dressed, and true to his word, Desmond didn't meet the day until he had. Then Desmond took the quarter hour he needed to get up off the floor.

Once upright, Desmond paced to get everything loose and in sync, and he wandered to the door in the course of his travels and peeked out through the door light.

"Hmm," Desmond said. "Dale's down there talking to Pearl."

"Just Dale?" I eased over to join Desmond at the door.

"Looks like it."

Pearl was trying to insist a plastic container of leftover casserole on him. She'd press it in Dale's hand, and Dale would give it back. Dale pointed at the car shed as he spoke, and Pearl shook her head with some vigor before starting in on the casserole again.

"Put on your suit coat," I told Luther, and then motioned him over to the door. I pointed at Dale. "Make him think me and Desmond aren't in Mississippi anymore."

In some ways, Duboises are about as can-do as people can possibly get. True enough, they're usually can-do in a criminal direction, but it seemed worthwhile to try to harness that ingenuity for relative good.

"Whatever you do, don't let him come up here."

"I hear you, boss," Luther told me. Then he flung open the door and went clattering down the steps.

"Good morning, Miss Pearl!"

Desmond and I watched Luther prance across the driveway.

"He's a little light in the tap shoes, wouldn't you say? I mean," Desmond added, "for a Dubois."

"Can a Dubois be gay and live to enjoy it?"

Desmond paused to consider the strife and trouble a gay Dubois would meet with. He shook his head and told me firmly, "Naw."

We couldn't hear Dale or Pearl, not enough to make out what they said, but Luther was so loud that everything he told them carried. His was a good story, as spontaneous bullshit goes. Me and Desmond had picked up and gone to Texas, and Luther had come into my lease. He was helping Pearl around the place and making himself useful for rent consideration and for clothes. At that point Luther showed Dale his sateen jacket lining.

"Isn't that Desmond's car out front?" Dale asked Luther with some volume, like maybe he suspected we were listening to him up top.

I looked around to see where we might go to if we had to. There was a knee wall back near the kitcheonette with a hole cut in it, access to an attic space covered with a plywood door. We could punch through the ceiling of Gil's garage and conceivably get out through there.

Desmond followed my gaze and told me, "Uh-uh."

"You'll fit," I said.

"Ain't about fitting. I don't go in attics. I don't go in basements. I don't go in bayous. I don't go in the woods."

"Doesn't leave much."

"I go to work. I go to the Sonic. I go home. If he comes up here, we'll just put him down again."

But the longer Dale stayed, the better Luther got. He'd come into Desmond's Metro on account of money Desmond owed for medicine (Luther called it) that Luther had supplied him for his mother. Apparently Dale was acquainted with Desmond's momma's pain.

"How did they go, then?" Dale wanted to know.

"Took the Amtrak out of Greenwood. Had tickets clear down to McComb. Catching a bus from there."

"Where in Texas?" Dale asked him.

Luther shrugged. "Big place," he said.

Dale couldn't seem to quite decide who to be angry with since me and Desmond were Galveston way and no longer handy for it. Then Luther bailed him out by poking Dale's bandage and asking him, "What's that?"

Dale picked Luther up by Gil's lapels and whispered something in Luther's ear. It was surely a threat against (knowing Dale) Luther's testicles. That was usually the part of a man, Mexican or otherwise, Dale could be relied on to threaten first.

"I'm watching you," Dale told Luther, but Luther was smoothing his lapels by then and seemed the sort who'd welcome watching by anyone who'd care to do it.

Pearl offered Dale the casserole again, and this time he took it and thanked her. So Dale would know a day of supplements and Skoal along with carrots and peas and chicken under a cheese potato chip crust.

When me and Desmond ride around together, we just climb in and go. There's no hold up for the one of us while the other gets himself ready, and we don't usually talk about where we're going or how we're going to get there. We just get in the car and figure it out en route.

That morning the job was to get to Webb and find the house Percy Dwayne had in mind, long before he would expect us to have arrived. Then we could see what was what and maybe figure who was who and decide where we needed to be to keep the whole thing from going sour.

Luther, however, was a Dubois and didn't know recon from études. Worse still, he was a clothes horse with an entire wardrobe for the taking, and Desmond and I were long since ready to roll while Luther was deciding what to wear.

What, after all, does a Yazoo drug slinger wear to a crack house in Webb? Particularly if the visit isn't attached to standard commerce but is more of a freelance SWATTY sort of thing. He just couldn't settle on an outfit to suit him, and Pearl was delighted to help him dither because the longer Luther took, the more insisting she could do.

We let them go on for a bit because Desmond and I had eased down into Pearl's house and were watching Dale watching the Geo from a block and a half away.

"Think we can wait him out?" Desmond wanted to know

"I don't know. He looks pretty comfortable."

Just then Barry White set in from Desmond's front shirt pocket. "It's you," he told me, and handed me the phone.

I hit the talk button. "Yeah," was all I had occasion to say before Percy Dwayne, sounding a little rattled, barked out, "Where's your goddamn charger?"

"For the phone?"

"Well, yeah," he told me in a tone that left me itching to

smack him, not that I wasn't already consumed with those
sorts of urges, anyway.

"It's here."

"That don't help me, now does it?"

"Can't imagine what I was thinking, not leaving it in the
car."

"How's this?" Luther asked me from the doorway in his
Sonny Crockett linen jacket and a Creamsicle undershirt.
Yazoo City Vice.

"Who's that?" Percy Dwayne wanted to know.

"Fellow at work," I told him.

"He the one bringing you over here?"

"Yeah. I guess."

"Good. You tell him to stay in the car and keep his goddamn mouth shut. And don't bring that big nigger, that other
repo boy."

"Why not?"

Percy Dwayne went irate. "'Cause I said so!" he screamed
at me.

"You're sounding a little jumpy."

"Just show up with the money. Don't you worry about me."

"And my car?"

"I'll call you and tell you where to find it. So bring the
charger, why don't you. I've just got two fucking bars."

"Noonish, right?"

And it sounded like Percy Dwayne was trying to correct
me on the time when he went all garbled and the connection
died.

"He didn't sound too good," I said to Desmond. "Didn't sound good at all."

Dale was still sitting up the road by the time Luther was dressed and ready to go, so me and Desmond really didn't have any choice but to trust Luther.

"You get the car, drive it down past Dale's cruiser, and get out on the truck route. Lose him but good. We'll cut through the back and meet you over by the Sunflower Market, far side near the dumpster."

"Keys?"

Desmond was having difficulty digging them out of his pocket. It was more of a mental than a motor skill sort of thing. He'd already been forced to surrender his Escalade to Shawnica, and now here I was asking him to hand the key to his Metro to a Dubois.

For a decent sort like Desmond, that was bound to be a bit of a hurdle. I talked him through it like I was his 12-step sponsor, and he finally handed his key ring to Luther with no comment beyond a grunt.

Luther tossed the ring in the air, all jaunty and delighted. He was like a shut-in on an outing. Every little thing he did in the fresh air was just fine with him.

Desmond grunted again, and we made our apologies to Pearl for the imposition, but she treated us like she was sending her boys off to school. She'd even bagged lunches for us and gave each of us a sack.

"What did you get?" Luther wanted to know before we were out of the house entirely.

I glanced in my sack. "Some kind of sandwich."

Luther poked me with his elbow. "I got a cupcake, too."

He headed down the driveway, fairly skipping, while me and Desmond made our way toward the back of the lot.

"Did you get a cupcake?" I asked Desmond.

He shook his head and exhaled hard. "Carrot sticks," he said.

The neighbor off the back had some kind of short-haired dog with three legs and one eye and a sour disposition. He looked like a veteran of the Great War. I knew him a little. His name was Rusty. I'd made his acquaintance a few months back when he'd spent about thirty-six straight hours barking at a stump. I think Rusty's remaining eye was clouded with cataracts, and just generally Rusty had lost all interest in caring what was what.

So he barked at stumps, would howl at nothing much in the middle of the day, and he didn't bother to squat anymore when he evacuated but would just lumber around shitting on everything.

He was a harmless canine geriatric, but Desmond was still scared of him and refused to pass through the gate between Pearl's lot and Rusty's yard. That meant I had to go in first and drive Rusty out of the way.

Since he was interested in my bag lunch, I went ahead and lured Rusty with it, tempting him away from the gate and across the yard. Desmond crossed and cleared the property while I was busy feeding the dog, pinching off bits of the sandwich Pearl had made.

She'd used pickle-pimento loaf, even though it was green around the edges, and the bread was slathered with mayonnaise Pearl had probably had for years. It was greasy translucent and what struck me as a toxic shade of yellow. The chips in their separate Baggie at the bottom of the sack were casserole rejects and largely salt and crumbs.

"He's going to be there, right?" Desmond asked me once I'd caught up with him.

I'd been wondering the same thing myself. We'd as good as kidnapped Luther and knocked him around a little, had hauled him up Delta, and gotten him compensated with Gil's clothes. But he was still a Dubois, and now he had a car. Who was to say he wouldn't head south toward Yazoo and disappear?

"He'll be there," I assured Desmond, but I didn't quite believe it.

We stuck to people's lawns and dodged between magnolia trees, keeping as best we could an eye out for Dale and his friends. When we got to the truck route, we hung around the Sunoco for a few minutes until a gap in the traffic provided us ample clearance to cross the road, and we passed through the lot at Fred's Pharmacy and approached the Sunflower Market. Then we stood for a solid half hour alongside the rank dumpster with no sign of Desmond's Metro anywhere.

"How stupid are we?" Desmond asked me just before Luther whipped into the lot. It wasn't all joy and relief, however, because he crossed the apron at such speed as to make sparks off Desmond's undercarriage.

"I'll undo anything he's done when this is all over," I told Desmond.

Desmond gave me a "Hmm." He added beyond it, "When's that going to be?"

It turned out Luther had stopped by the Krystal and bought himself a Scrambler, which was eggs and pancakes and sausage all shoved in a Styrofoam cup. Not the sort of meal you could hope to eat behind the wheel of a Metro, but Luther had given it a vigorous go nonetheless.

So he had a fair bit of syrup and sausage grease on his Creamsicle shirt and scattershot Scrambler detritus on his lap and down on the floorboard. It looked a little like he'd taken fire in the form of a breakfast grenade.

"Look at this," Desmond said, disgusted at the mess.

Luther paid him no mind at all, but just stood by the dumpster eating his Scrambler with the spork he'd been provided, which appeared to work about half as well as a genuine fork or spoon.

"I'm sorry," I told him as I helped Desmond pick up and tidy his car.

"They ain't like us," he said, and glanced at Luther, who, standing right beside a dumpster, finished his breakfast and dropped his Styrofoam cup onto the ground.

"Pick that up," I told him.

"I was aiming to do that," Luther said.

Luther picked up his Scrambler cup and his napkin and his spork and just stood there with them in his hand until I'd pointed out the dumpster right beside him. He dropped them in with an air of rank experimentation like he'd never contemplated such a thing before.

Luther complained bitterly about riding in the back. His coat would get all wrinkled and he had less room than before because now he was sharing his cramped space with a shotgun and a box of shells.

Desmond asked me if he could stop by his house and check in on his momma, by which I figured he meant he wanted to see after her pain. He had Luther's grimy tablets in his shirt pocket with his phone, and they weren't doing his mother awfully much good there.

Desmond had grown up and lived on the banks of the Big Sunflower River, out in the country north of Indianola between Dwyer and Pentecost.

Desmond's father had owned what, anywhere else, would have been a nice parcel of farmland. A couple of hundred acres of Big Sunflower River bottom that he'd even farmed for a decade or two before his neighbor bought him out. His neighbor was a multinational conglomerate operating out of Denmark. His neighbor had eighty thousand acres of Delta under plow.

The house Desmond now shared with his mother was like a wealth of houses in the Delta. It was located snug by the street where the rows would have ended, anyway, so it could be graciously tolerated for now, agriculturally speaking. It got crop dusted probably half the year, and when the fields were burned in the fall, Desmond stayed home with his mother just in case the wind backed on them. It was the sort of house indifference and poor luck would probably sweep away in a few years.

Desmond's father had built it, and like I said, Desmond's father was a farmer, so it looked like a house a farmer had built on those occasions the crops allowed. Frame. Asbestos shingles. Metal roof with tires to hold it down. An addition out back that still had more house wrap exposed than siding. An outhouse that saw use when the plumbing froze or happened to get cocked up.

"Want to come in?" Desmond asked me, but I'd been in once before and didn't think Desmond needed me there just now.

"We'll stay out here. Give my best to your mom."

Me and Luther just stood in the yard. A May breeze was driving the bugs away, and high clouds were drifting in from Arkansas. The Big Sunflower was flowing on the far side of the road. It was silty and slow and about as far as a river can get from majestic. There was a black kid shin-deep on the far side fishing, I guess, for carp.

Luther took a long look upstream and then downstream for a while, and, when he turned to me to speak, I thought for a second he might say something profound. Well, not profound in the usual sense but relative to Dubois standards. I hoped some cracker Delta insight might just spill out of his mouth.

Instead, gazing at the Big Sunflower had brought him to this: "Now I've got to take a piss."

"Outhouse around back," I told him.

"Snakes love them damn things," he said. So I pointed him toward the sandy lot up the road from Desmond's house where his Danish conglomerate neighbors stored their implements under a shed, a shed about the size of a shopping plaza.

Luther peed on a six-foot harrow blade and seemed delighted for the chance.

Standing alone in Desmond's yard, I was aware of a brand of sensation that I'd known a time or two in the Delta before. Big sky overhead. Shabby little house. Muddy implacable river. Soybeans stretching to the horizon. A line of power poles was the tallest thing around, and the soil beneath them had been plowed so much that they were all pitched and tilted.

The fields were massive. The tractors were huge. The scale was so off in the Delta that people seemed smaller than life.

Standing there in Desmond's yard, I got a whiff of fruitlessness. I was touched by the passing conviction that a niggling sort like me would never make anything happen quite the way I wanted to. I was left to wonder what sense it possibly made to try. That view of the world is as much of the Delta as the black loam and the mosquitoes. I felt it only briefly, the way a transplant would, but it made me appreciate Desmond more for staying upright and decent, and it helped explain why a creature like Luther was bound to be who he was.

When people toss off how the Delta is damned, they're just talking shorthand. The Delta's less a place than a boot on your neck. The Delta keeps you down.

ELEVEN

To get to Webb, we went north to Parchman to cut east on 32. But for the main penitentiary gate, the prison looks like an airbase. Like everything else in the Delta, Parchman's a farm as well, and the convicts who aren't working the land are often out tidying roadsides. They wear striped fatigues. Green and white, broad stripes like a barbershop awning. The guards carry shotguns and are always in campaign hats against the sun.

"Ever been inside?" I asked Desmond, but before he could tell me, Luther set about listing all the friends he had in Parchman, a few of them he wasn't even related to.

"You go see them?"

Luther's mouth fell open, and he looked at me like I was

daft. "In there?" He pointed as we turned right at the imposing main prison gate. "What if I couldn't get back out?"

"I don't think that's how it works."

"Does down here," Luther insisted, and Desmond grunted as if to say he'd found a thing he could finally agree with a Dubois about.

Route 32 covered about eight miles of what looked like solid wheat with a shack or three to serve as crop-duster targets. It dead-ended into what is officially known as the Emmett Till Highway, but K-Lo was the only person I'd ever heard call it that. He'd hit his bobcat on the Emmett Till Highway, somewhere near Glendora, so it figured in the story he liked to tell about that night, which was colorful and thorough but for the part about his car. Like most everybody else in the Delta, K-Lo didn't know who Emmett Till was.

The courthouse still stands up in Sumner, where the men who murdered that child were acquitted. I can hardly ever drive past a bayou without thinking of that poor boy's body sunk in the mud barbwired to a cotton gin fan.

Webb was hardly a mile up his road, and we eased in from the south on a back way Desmond was acquainted with. I had to think Desmond had probably bought some medicine in Webb at one time or another. From the looks of the place, that was the leading brand of commerce about.

I don't know if Webb had ever been much, but it sure was nothing now. There was a kind of shack suburb on the low end of town, and we passed directly through it. Dirt yards and clothes hanging out to dry on bushes and fence rails mostly. I had to get out to physically roust a dog from the middle of the street.

"Is our house around here?" I asked Desmond.

"Naw," he said dismissively as if the place we were going to, still a Delta drug den, was in a far nicer neighborhood than the one we were rolling through.

"Damned if I know how people live like this." That was Luther from the back.

I told him we'd been to his house on Longstreet Street, and it wasn't exactly palatial.

"Got a new place," Luther told me. "Up near Norway. Grass in the yard and everything. Nothing like this here."

And it was a stricken sort of place as Delta neighborhoods go. Blighted and tumbledown with the occasional over-accessorized car. Then we passed through downtown Webb, which was hardly any better. It had the layout and look of a lot of Delta towns I'd seen. A couple of blocks of brick storefronts, maybe a feed-and-seed still open, and usually a Mexican grocery store somewhere in the mix, but otherwise just dusty plate glass and desolation.

Webb was uncommon, though, in the volume of people just loitering about. Black men primarily, though a few toddlers and infants, too, and some women mixed in doing just as little as the men. That was the thing. They weren't talking or eating or drinking. They weren't doing anything but looking at us as they parted to let us pass.

"I guess everybody knows we're here," I said.

"That boy back there in the dashiki," Desmond told me.

It was brown and orange and yellow. I couldn't help but see him myself. "It's his house we're going to. Everything that comes to Webb goes right through him."

"Who is he?"

"Calvin."

"Calvin? Doesn't he have a badass, dope-slinging name? I mean . . . Calvin?"

"Got some Swahili bullshit name nobody'll call him."

"Is he the boy that cut off that guy's thumb?" Luther asked. He turned full around to study Calvin in his autumn-shade dashiki.

"That's him," Desmond said.

"Who's thumb?"

"Guy from Helena, right?" Luther said.

"Uh-huh," Desmond told him.

"In a fight?"

"Naw," Desmond told me. "I hear he was asleep. Think somebody bet him he wouldn't."

"Damn. People around here and their knives," I said, and looked as directly at Luther as I could manage.

"I ain't never stuck nobody but him," Luther said, "and he flat told me to."

"Hmm."

"You were bad back then," Luther told Desmond. "Don't guess I was much better."

"But we're all fine now," I offered, "which is how we ended up here."

Desmond pointed out a house, a little square thing with

purple siding and wooden goose wind vane driven on a stake into the yard. He kept going and swung around the corner, did a four-point road turn, and parked.

"Where did he want it?"

"Porch was all he said. Front one, I guess. What time is it?"

"About ten of twelve," Desmond told me.

"I'll carry it over. Think we're all right here?"

Desmond wasn't so sure. He sized up the houses in the vicinity and selected one with gladiolus in the yard and a rocker on the porch.

Desmond climbed out of the Geo, went up and knocked on the door. A tiny, gray-haired, nut-colored lady showed up behind the screen. I watched Desmond gain her permission to back his Geo into her drive. He gave her three dollars and told her we worked for the CIA.

Once we'd backed in and were set where we could see down the road through her shrubbery, she brought us out ice water and told us about her brother's wife, who was cleaning out her brother's bank account and making her brother's life a torment. She wondered what the CIA might have to say about that.

At ten after noon precisely, I left the car and walked over to Calvin's. Unlike on Main Street in downtown Webb, there wasn't anybody about. A cat crossed the road ahead of me, and a dog barked at me from a window. I don't suspect I'll ever feel so lily white again.

There wasn't any Calvin around. Wasn't any Dubois. Just me and my sack of newsprint cut up to look like dollar bills.

I climbed Calvin's steps and listened at the door. The house sounded empty to me. I set my bag on the porch decking, opened the neck, and arranged all the twenties to show. Then I rolled the sack shut, left Calvin's porch, and returned to Desmond's car.

"Now what?" Luther wanted to know.

"We wait for Percy Dwayne or . . . somebody."

"Then what?"

"I get Pearl's car back. Beat up your uncle a little. You go back to your office. Me and him go back to work."

"Nobody goes to jail?"

"I can't see how that would help."

"Well, you're all right then," Luther told me, "for somebody from somewhere else."

A good half hour passed before we saw anybody.

"Right there," Desmond said, and he pointed at a lanky kid walking up the street.

The guy was glancing all over while trying to seem to be looking at nothing much. He stopped in front of Calvin's house and made the worst fake phone call I ever hope to see a human make. It was somewhere between Vicksburg dinner theater and a middle-school Thanksgiving play.

He laughed and hooted and looked one last time up and down the road before he dashed up onto Calvin's porch, nabbed the sack, and dashed back off it.

He unrolled the neck and took a long, hard look inside. I held my breath a little until he'd rolled the neck back shut and set out down the street. From the constipated way he moved, he appeared to have been instructed that he damn well better not do anything to draw attention to himself.

He was walking away toward the head of the road, and we just watched him there at first until he left the pavement and climbed a hill through a patch of scrub and saplings. Only then did Desmond wheel out into the street and roll up to the end of the block where he let me out of the car.

"We'll go around," he said, and left me to follow the guy on foot.

I went up the scrubby hill, paused at the top, and found myself looking at the back of a makeshift church. The place appeared to have started as warehouse before it got sanctified. I saw a flash of shirt as that boy with the bag ducked around the far corner.

I could hear him before I saw him. This time he was making an actual call.

"Got it," he said. "I'm here."

Then he got talked at for a bit. I took a peek at him around the corner of that warehouse church.

"Aw'ight," he said, and listened.

"Weren't nobody anywhere."

He got talked at some more. Instructed, I guess.

"Be there in five," he said.

Then he crossed the road, cut through a lot, and I just stood and watched him from the corner of the holiness warehouse.

When Desmond came rolling up, I pointed to show him where to go. I crossed the road and entered the lot, passed through to the next block over, and saw that boy with the sack go in some manner of half-assed restaurant.

It had a Royal Crown Cola sign in the window. The whole place was painted chartreuse. I could smell the fry oil before I saw the hand-lettered box bottom taped to the door. CATFISH, it read. CHICKEN. RIBS.

Desmond pulled up, and him and Luther climbed out of the Geo. I told them, "Stay here," and tapped on my chest to let them know this thing was mine.

I'm not quite sure what I expected to find once I'd opened the door and gone in. Maybe that Dubois. Maybe that Vardaman. Maybe even the both of them with their stinky kid. Instead I got the Webb cartel eating catfish nuggets and drinking Pepsis. Calvin had the prime seat over in the corner, and he was looking in the sack when I came in.

Calvin had found his first stack of newsprint just as I entered the place.

Even in a dashiki and sitting down, Calvin proved capable of nearly dismantling the kid who'd brought him the sack. He punched him. He kicked him. He flung him to a colleague, who punched him and kicked him and tossed him around some more. Then he noticed me.

"This you?" Calvin asked me, pointing at the sack.

I nodded.

"Then we've got a problem."

"Don't see how."

"Your asshole owes me. He says you owe him. That means you owe me. See it now?"

"What's between you and him is between you and him. All I know is that shithead stole my car. Where is he?"

"Fuck you, Homer." With that, Calvin started fishing from the sack neat bundles of fake cash and throwing them at me. One at a time, and with considerable leisure and toothy smirks all around. They bounced off me and dropped to the floor. Then he balled up the empty bag and threw that, too.

"So?" he said.

"My wallet's in the car," I told him. "I'll be right back, and you and me'll settle up."

I don't know if they thought I was spooked and intimidated or they just didn't give a shit, but they let me walk out of there. I went straight to the Geo and pulled the shotgun out, grabbed a fistful of shells, and shoved them in as Desmond and Luther watched.

"Everything okay?" Desmond asked.

I nodded and told him, "Peachy."

Luther wondered if, while I was in there, I'd pick him up an order of ribs.

I stepped inside and told those fellows, "Now then."

I wasn't angry. I don't believe I was even much in the way of agitated. I'd just reached that point where I was through doing things like I'd done them before. Everybody stopped eating, and Calvin wiped his fingers on a napkin. He smiled like a man who's seen the wrong end of a shotgun once or twice.

"Can't shoot us all," he told me.

"I can sure as shit try."

There were six of us in there altogether, not counting the

boy who'd brought the bag and the woman over at the Fryolator.

"You two might want to clear out," I said, and they welcomed the chance to do it, while the guy to Calvin's immediate right, who was big and looked dead stupid, started groping for whatever gangster hardware he had shoved in his pants.

I took a quick step toward him and tapped his forehead with the shotgun butt. He said some version of "Umph" and dropped face-first to the table.

The three other colleagues started squirming, and I told them all, "Stay put."

Two of them did, but one of them bolted for the door. I heard him run into Desmond and Luther together and at once. From the sound of it he got put down hard and then tap-danced on with vigor.

"You," I said to Calvin, "come here."

Calvin had been watching entirely too much cop-show television. He had the lines down, though I can't quite say how he'd ended up in a dashiki. He seemed confused about where his heritage and his methamphetamines met. But he knew what to say, and he stayed right in his chair and said it.

"I'm happy enough," he told me, "where I am."

It was almost like he thought I lacked the nerve to change his mind. If he'd caught me a few months earlier, I might have let it go, would have probably figured his taste in outerwear was punishment enough. At that moment, though, I'd lost my talent for accommodation.

The nexus between Aw-fuck-it and I-don't-give-shit is a beautiful place to be. I could see that in an instant because I'd lost all sense of consequences. I was right there with Calvin exclusively, needing from him what I needed, and it didn't matter to me if I shot him or beat him or took him out for brunch.

I didn't particularly want him dead, but if Calvin got that way, I wasn't prepared to worry much about it.

That sort of attitude tends to come off a fellow like a scent, and Calvin knew enough wanna-be gangsters to recognize the difference. For appearance's sake, however, he needed to let me hit him once. I settled on a fist this time instead of K-Lo's shotgun butt, caught Calvin square in the jaw, and sent him tumbling onto the floor. One of his buddies eyeballed me so that I gave him the gun butt instead.

"On the floor," I told the last one, who still had his wits about him.

He went down stomach first on that nasty rolled linoleum— all grease and grit and years of stark neglect—and I relieved him of what turned out to be a knockoff Desert Eagle.

I drew open the slide and the whole thing fell apart. Made in North Korea or somewhere. There were two bullets in the clip and more rust on the works than you'd find on most backyard grills.

"What kind of thug are you?" I asked him.

Beyond calling me "sir" and making apologetic noises, he didn't appear to have much interest in what kind of thug he was.

"Go on," I told him, and I shouted out the door so could pass untapped on and get away.

"You want to give me a hand?" I said to Luther, who poked his head into the place and came fully inside once he was sure it was only me left standing.

"We're taking him," I said of Calvin.

"Okay," Luther told me, but he went straight behind the counter to collect his takeout order of ribs. He ate a couple in the process and sang the praises of them, came over, and wiped his greasy hands on Calvin's dashiki as we were lifting him up.

It turned out Calvin had a Steyr TMP under his dashiki, the 9-mm machine pistol. The thing knocked against me when I picked him up. He was wearing it on a strap, and it was all cocked and loaded. Oiled and cared for. Babied, even. When I handed it over to Desmond, Calvin actually stamped his feet.

"Bad day, bubby?" I asked him.

He spat on the ground much in the style of K-Lo's lovely wife.

I doubt the engineers who'd designed Desmond's Metro (not that I'm sure there were any) ever imagined there'd be much need for your standard Metro owner to load up three of his full-sized colleagues and drive them all over the place.

Given the way Desmond's driver's seat was backed clean off the rails, there wasn't much for Luther to do but sit on top of Calvin. Calvin raised a considerable fuss about that.

He got all drug-lordy on us, asking us all those questions

kingpins ask. Did we know who he was? Did we know who his friends were? Did we know what they could do to us?

Luther removed one of Gil's tap shoes and beat Calvin on his cowlick until Calvin grew meek and finally shut up.

"Where's Percy Dwayne?" I asked him

"Cocksucker owes me money."

"Five thousand dollars? Bullshit. You'd never let him in that deep."

Calvin didn't say anything, just grunted and looked sullen.

I glanced at Luther, who smacked Calvin cowlick again.

"Two thousand! I sold him a car."

"When?"

"Yesterday."

"That's funny," I said, "because I kind of sold him a car yesterday, too."

"Wasn't driving nothing when I saw him."

"When was that?"

"Afternoon. Three. Maybe four."

"He coming for the other three thousand?"

"Taking it to him. In dope."

"Is Percy Dwayne going into business?" I asked him.

"Seems so," Calvin told me.

"And you don't mind?"

"Shit kickers down yonder? I don't give a damn."

"Did you know about this?" I asked Luther.

He shook his head. "Percy Dwayne slings it sometimes. Usually after that wife of his has had enough of his laying around."

"Where are you meeting him?" I asked Calvin.

"No damn where," he told me. "Ain't no money. Sure as shit ain't going to be no dope."

"Don't you want your car back?"

Calvin shook his head.

"Wasn't yours to start with?"

Calvin grunted.

"Well, there's going to be a meeting," I told him. "Money or no money, so where are we going?"

"Why the fuck should I tell you any goddamn thing?"

Luther tapped Calvin on top of his head because the moment impressed him as fitting.

"Ow!" Calvin said. "Quit it!"

"Where are you meeting him?" I asked.

Calvin went sullen. Luther tapped him again.

"Greenwood," he told us. "Over at the Sonic."

Desmond had only been drifting and whistling until then, but he came awfully close to squealing with delight.

TWELVE

So back down the Emmett Till Highway we went, riding low and chugging along as fast as four cylinders could take us. All I know is we were lucky that the Delta is dead flat or we'd have met every incline by bailing out to push.

Calvin had to pee the whole way and complained bitterly about it. He went on at length about how it didn't much help his bladder to have a cracker sitting right on top of him. That just prompted Luther to poke and antagonize Calvin all the more.

Of course, Luther was naturally curious about Calvin's taste in clothes since a dashiki seemed to him the sort of thing you'd wear around the house. Luther couldn't imagine throwing one on and going out for lunch. Even in Webb.

Calvin thought Luther was just having some white trash fun at his expense, but Luther's interest seemed genuine and strictly sartorial. It didn't help that Luther was eating ribs pretty much on top of Calvin and that Luther didn't appear to care where the grease ran or the sauce happened to drip.

The Cottonlandia Museum is directly across the truck route from the Greenwood Sonic. Desmond pulled into the lot there and probably gave the staff a thrill. How many visitors can a museum devoted to cotton picking get? But we didn't climb out, just sat and surveyed the cars lined up for service at the Sonic. Luther allowed Calvin to sit full upright and look out the Metro windshield.

"That one," he said, and pointed to a battered blue sedan. It was dinged all over, rusted at the fenders, and about as filthy as a car could be.

"You're getting two thousand for that?" Desmond asked.

And Calvin got all shirty. "For a fellow with no money and no credit at all, two thousand ain't too damn bad."

"Let's go over there." I pointed out a spot near the Sonic building proper where Desmond never parked because of the greasy cooktop exhaust.

He shot me a look to remind me about it.

"Just for a minute," I told him. "We'll swap out Calvin for Percy Dwayne, and then head out into the country to chat him up."

"How am I supposed to get home?" Calvin wanted to know.

"In your car," I told him, and pointed.

"It's stole!" he reminded me.

"Drive the limit. You'll be fine."

Desmond made a trial run by the Sonic to see if there were any any police about on the lookout for his Metro. Pinhead friends of Dale's hoping to settle the score. There was a county cruiser parked up at the end of the car hop bays, but once we were satisfied it was only Kendell, Desmond pulled on in, like I'd suggested, beneath the cooktop vent.

"He's all mine," I said. I grabbed the fireplace shovel off the floorboard, climbed out of the Geo, and eased behind the cars between us and Percy Dwayne. The girl was just bringing Percy Dwayne's order as I was closing on him, so I lingered behind a panel truck until she'd fixed the tray to his door.

He'd gone heavy. A holster of popcorn chicken. A corn dog. A double order of chili cheese Tater Tots. A gigantic blue coconut slush to wash it down. It was a hell of a lunch, but I doubted anything could impede my swing.

I let him start in. He popped a tot and a couple of chicken nuggets. He had the corn dog in his mouth when I stepped up alongside him.

His eyes got big, and he looked like he was primed to start explaining, but a mouth full of corn dog prevented him from it. That and a shovel blow to the forehead.

I swung through his lunch. Björn Borg again. Percy Dwayne's gigantic coconut blue slush particularly went flying. Chili cheese Tater Tots scattered to the hinterlands as well. He spat a little corn dog coating my way and then slumped against the wheel.

I lifted the tray from his door and chucked the whole

thing into a trash barrel, waved Desmond over, and he rolled up just behind that Dubois's car. Desmond and Luther and Calvin all piled out of the Metro, and we hoisted Percy Dwayne and delivered him to the Geo floorboard. Then Calvin set in to complaining about the mess I'd made in his stolen coupe that he was going to have to drive clear back to Webb. There was chili and coconut blue slush all over the place but for a little ass-shaped spot where Percy Dwayne had been sitting.

"Stay right there," I said to Calvin. "You'll be fine."

He sneered my way as he slipped in under the wheel. Calvin hardly let Desmond pull clear before he backed out and roared off.

I glanced over and saw that Kendell was drinking a cup of Sonic coffee and watching every little thing we did. I felt like I owed him an explanation, him being reliable police and all, so I started toward his cruiser with that fireplace shovel still in hand.

"Don't want to know," Kendell told me as I approached his open window. "Going to see the chiropractor. Don't have time to arrest all you today."

Desmond blew the horn of his Geo. I told Kendell so long, went back to the car, and climbed in the front seat. We rolled on out of the Sonic. It seemed the sensible thing to do. I'm sure that was the first time Desmond had ever left a Sonic unfed.

We carried Percy Dwayne to the sea of cotton warehouses just south of Greenwood on the old Yazoo City road. Once we'd parked back among them where nobody was likely to stumble across us, we pulled that Dubois from the car and laid him out on the pea gravel, stood around, and waited for him to wake up.

"Why's he all blue?" Luther wanted to know.

"Coconut slush," Desmond told him. "That ain't no drink for a man."

The warehouses all around us were packed to the rafters with unsold bales of cotton, and the doors were all flung open to keep them dry and sound. According to Desmond, the price was so low that it would have been foolish to sell, so all the cotton in the Delta was just piling up until the stuff became more dear.

I went over and fiddled with a bale, pulled out a tuft, and worked it in my hands. Cotton makes sense when you see it like that. All ginned and soft and fluffy. It's the stuff in the fields that's hateful.

When I first saw cotton in season, I pulled off the road by a patch of it and waded out to pick a little, just a bole or three. That was all it took to bring me to a fresh opinion of Delta slavery.

It hadn't been just farm work in diabolical heat. It was harvesting this evil stuff, with spikes on the boles to prick your fingers and the plant growing precisely low enough to make you sorry you had a spine. Cotton is agriculture as punishment, and now they couldn't even sell it, which seemed fitting if only a hundred and fifty years too late.

That fireplace shovel had raised a purple welt smack in

the middle of Percy Dwayne's forehead. Sprawled on the ground there he looked like a white trash unicorn at rest. He stayed out for about a quarter hour, and while we waited for him to come around, Desmond reminded me every way possible that he was just at a Sonic and hadn't gotten the chance to eat.

"We'll take care of that," I kept telling him, but he was kind of in shock. Parked at a Sonic without so much as a bite of a Coney Island.

"I was right there," Desmond told me.

"I know," I said. "We'll fix it."

Percy Dwayne finally stirred and woke. He groaned and looked up at us. Me and Desmond didn't interest him much, but Luther snared his attention.

"I'll kill you," were the first words Percy Dwayne bothered to say.

"He don't mean it," Luther told us.

"If you say so." Then I gave Percy Dwayne a poke in the ribs. "Remember me?"

He favored me with a look of high theatrical bemusement. "Uh-uh," he said, so I tapped him with the shovel just like he'd done me the day before.

"All right, all right. It's all coming back."

"Get up."

He made five minutes of groaning labor out of just standing from the ground. Then the fool tried to bolt, and Desmond put a shoulder in him and knocked him back over. I tapped him again with the shovel, just because.

"Where's my car?" I asked him.

"Where's my money?" he wanted to know.

"Explain to him," I said to Luther, "I'll make his brains leak out of his ears."

And Luther turned toward Percy Dwayne and opened his mouth to speak, but Percy Dwayne headed him off by reminding Luther, "I'll kill you."

"Where's my car?"

Percy Dwayne indulged in what I believed to be stalling, which I decided to take as provocation for further shovel blows.

"Where is it?"

That's when he told me about the worst thing I could hear. "I don't know," Percy Dwayne said.

"Hold this," I told Desmond, and gave him the shovel.

I grabbed Percy Dwayne by his damp blue shirtfront and helped him up off the ground so I could pitch him into the corrugated warehouse siding.

"Where is it?" I asked him.

He wouldn't talk, just shook his head and dithered, so I smacked him once across the jaw with the back of my open hand.

"Did you sell it?"

"Uh-uh."

"Then where is it?"

"I kind of gave it to a guy."

"That doesn't sound like you. Does that sound like him?"

Luther told me it didn't sound like Percy Dwayne at all.

"What guy?"

He stalled again, and I cocked my fist but didn't hit him.

"Bad guy," Percy Dwayne told me.

"You gave it to him or he took it?"

Percy Dwayne nodded, which I found unhelpful, so I did in fact hit him again.

"Couldn't we be doing all this over at the Sonic?" Desmond wanted to know.

Desmond wouldn't settle for anything less than the Indianola Sonic, and Percy Dwayne rode over folded up between Luther and Desmond's shoulder. He whined most of the way over, told us how the world was stacked against him. Percy Dwayne had a thing for going around wounded all the time. Everybody owed him something. We'd all made out but him. There's no telling what heights he could have scaled if the world didn't have it in for him.

I didn't have to hit him once he'd started with that crap. Desmond knocked him silly before he could even get moaning good. Desmond was a 350-pound black man in the Mississippi Delta. If the world was stacked against somebody, it was more than likely him.

Percy Dwayne had the gall to ask me to replace his lunch. Luther, in the way of a peace offering, bought his uncle another corn dog, but chili cheese Tater Tots didn't strike Luther as food any sane man would eat. That chafed Percy Dwayne, who was hardly hoping for dietary advice from Luther, and they got into a family spat all piled up in the Geo's backseat.

Desmond's preferred space was down at the end of the car hop line facing back toward the corner of the redwood fence that separated the Sonic from the duplex shared by the Long John Silver and the Taco Bell. This was Desmond's Zen garden. Three Coney Islands and a sunny day and Desmond was about as close to heaven on earth as he might get.

He wasn't inclined to tolerate squabbling, preferred no speaking at all, and he certainly wouldn't take his lunch with chatter from Duboises, which Desmond conveyed to both of them together with the meaty palm of his hand.

"Shit, buddy!" Desmond had caught Percy Dwayne entirely by surprise. "Is knocking people around all you guys know?"

"That's rich," I told him, "coming from you."

"I needed my TV," Percy Dwayne said, almost by way of apology.

"All you had to do was pay on it."

"Things been tight," he whined.

I had to divide my attention between Percy Dwayne and keeping an eye out for Dale or his pinheaded colleagues on the Indianola PD.

"Now then," I said to Percy Dwayne once our food had come and Desmond was fully occupied with his condiment packets. "Where's my Ranchero?"

"I knew," Percy Dwayne said, "I should have stayed clear of that son of a bitch."

"Start at the beginning," I told Percy Dwayne, but it soon became plain he wasn't sure where the beginning might be.

"I know this guy down by Spanish Fort. Name's Eugene."

"I know him," Luther said. "Comes around selling shit sometimes," he told me. "You know—stole shit mostly."

"Stickiest goddamn fingers you ever seen," Percy Dwayne said. "So I'm down there around Rolling Fork getting some gas . . ." And here Percy Dwayne winked at me and grew vehicularly chummy. "That damn thing flat burns it," he said.

It hardly seemed worth the effort to smack him again.

"So I'm filling it up," Percy Dwayne told me, "and here comes Eugene in that piece-of-shit thing he drives. It's like four different trucks slapped together, and he hauls all his stole shit in it. Anyway, he sees that truck thing of yours."

"Ranchero," I told him.

"Yeah, that. And he gets all worked up about it because he says he knows this fellow that'd go flat to pieces for it. I can tell this is some guy Eugene's looking to get in with. So I ask him, 'Who is he?' But he won't say. Just tells me this guy'd probably give me real money for the thing."

"So you sold it?" Percy Dwayne was making me tired.

"I fucking wish. Went kind of crooked after that."

Percy Dwayne went back to his corn dog and gnawed on it with commitment until I snatched it from him and flung it out the window.

Then Desmond studied me in such a way as to make me understand he couldn't begin to countenance that sort of be-havior at a Sonic.

So I got out of the Geo, picked up that corn dog, and laid

it on the tray. Percy Dwayne was picking grit off it by the time I'd settled back into the car.

"Crooked how?" I asked him.

"Eugene wants me to follow him back to his place. I don't want to go there, and Sissy sure as shit ain't hoping to pay him a visit."

"Sissy?"

"The missus," Luther said.

"Eugene says this guy he knows'll pay real money for that Ranchero, and I don't want it really because—I'll tell you something—it ain't too awful good for much. Can't haul nothing. Carry maybe what? A quarter cord of wood? Ain't no kind of truck and too tight inside for a car. It's no wonder they don't make them anymore."

Eugene, as it turned out, lived in a house down on the False River that runs through the Delta National Forest. He was one of those mud cats with a place in the swamp, up on stilts and more or less out of the way of the alligators. Him or his people had been there a while with rights and claims and privileges, and as the national forest had grown and spread, it had just filled in around them.

"So you went to Eugene's place after all?" I asked Percy Dwayne.

He nodded and then managed an expression of considered regret, which I'd have to say is fairly rare for Delta cracker trash.

They'll regret taking a hit at the casino blackjack tables, and they'll sometimes regret being caught at a crime once they're on their way to Parchman, but Delta crackers as a rule are forward-looking people if by *forward-looking* you mean a scant ten minutes ahead.

"Yeah," Percy Dwayne said at last with something approaching rue. "We followed Eugene to his place." Then he shook his head and grunted—kind of a triumph for a Dubois without a gun pointed at him.

"Give me the short version," I suggested to Percy Dwayne.

"They got took," he told me.

"Who?"

"Sissy and PD Jr. Your goddamn Ranchero."

"Took?"

Percy Dwayne nodded.

"What exactly does that mean?"

"Eugene's buddy . . . who ain't Eugene's buddy . . . swooped in and got them all."

"Kidnapped?" I asked him.

"Ain't that what *took* means!?"

Now Percy Dwayne was making Desmond and Luther tired as well.

"Didn't I tell you," Percy Dwayne reminded us, "the whole goddamn thing went crooked?"

THIRTEEN

"Gee," he said. "You know, like Guy but Gee."

"He's French?" I asked Percy Dwayne.

He shook his head. "Some half-assed Acadian fuck stick."

"Tell me you ain't messing with *him!*" Luther was fairly shouting. As it turned out, he knew Percy Dwayne's half-assed Acadian fuck stick by his purely diabolical reputation. "Not that guy!"

"Gee," Percy Dwayne told him.

"Who is he?" By now I was more anxious to hear from Luther than his uncle. Luther at least knew how to tell a thing straight.

"Got run out of New Orleans. Feds or something. Set up down around Vicksburg. Been coming north ever since."

"What's his thing?'

"Meth mostly," Luther told me, "but he'll move whatever he can. Deep into hash and some kind of Ecstasy bullshit for a while. But he's cooking meth all over these days. Illegals do it for him."

"And he took my car?" I asked Percy Dwayne.

"And Sissy," he told me, "PD Jr., too."

"What the hell for? A meth dealer / kidnapper? Who has the fucking time?"

Percy Dwayne shrugged and then rubbed his fingers and thumb together. "Wants three thousand. And that's just for them. He's figuring on keeping the car."

Percy Dwayne didn't seem too bothered by the trouble his family was in.

"This guy ain't no damn good," Luther told me.

And Percy Dwayne said, "Gee."

"Calvin said you were taking drugs instead of money."

"Hoping to turn them around, make a little off the top." He sounded like a man whose wife was home in the kitchen making dinner.

"Heard of this guy?" I asked Desmond.

"Gee," Percy Dwayne said.

Desmond had finally gotten his Coney Islands dressed to suit him and decided to take a bite of it first and answer my question in time.

Desmond nodded. Desmond chewed. "Killed a boy I know."

"Really?"

"Must have," Desmond told me. "Nobody else needed him dead."

"You supposed to deliver the cash?"

Percy Dwayne nodded.

"When?"

"That ain't all worked out yet."

"You don't have the first fucking idea what you're up to, do you?" I said to Percy Dwayne.

Of course he got defensive and pitiful all at the same time. He knew just what he was doing and the world was stacked against him.

"You know how to reach this Guy?" I asked him.

"Through Eugene," he said.

"How are you going to reach Eugene?"

"I could call him, I guess, but your damn phone's near dead and it don't have none of my numbers in it." He said it like it was all my fault.

"You hearing this?" I asked Desmond.

Desmond held up a hand to suggest that he was unavailable at the moment. That he wasn't about to let any cracker fool spoil his Sonic lunch.

"We're just going to be quiet for a minute and let Desmond eat."

"My corn dog's got shit on it," Percy Dwayne told me, and showed me some corn dog grit.

"Shhhh," I said, and put a finger to my lips.

While I was waiting for Desmond to eat his lunch, I used the leisure to piece together Percy Dwayne's previous twenty-four hours, which had started off with me and him and that fireplace shovel. He'd then gone joyriding in a freshly stolen calypso coral Ranchero, had headed down to the southern Delta where Duboises were thick on the ground.

He'd then run by chance across Eugene at a Rolling Fork gas station, and Eugene had thrown him in with that evil Acadian fuck stick Guy, who'd taken his wife and his son and the car he'd originally stolen from me. Now he was hoping to buy them back or dope them up or something. I wasn't entirely clear on what he meant to do or why.

That was one full day, but I had to figure me and Desmond could match it. I'd started out on the wrong end of Percy Dwayne's late morning. We'd roughed up K-Lo, put Dale down, and let some Mexicans loose. Then we'd beat down a couple of fellows we didn't even know on Longstreet Street in beautiful Creekside Estates just outside Yazoo.

That had led us to Tootie's, where we'd packed Luther upside down on the back Geo floorboard. Then an evening featuring Angela Marie—and I dwelled on her for a moment—up in Memphis, in her office, being responsible and running things. K-Lo and his burglars seemed like it happened a year ago by now. A slumber party at my garage apartment, a trip to Webb. My new friend Calvin in his dashiki with an Austrian machine pistol underneath—about the last thing I expected to find in Webb.

And now me and Percy Dwayne had closed the circle—me without my TV payment and him without Gil's car.

I couldn't help but think how very different my twenty-four hours would have been if Percy Dwayne had just put down twenty dollars on his television or had even sat at his dinette with me and told me why he couldn't. I wondered what we'd be up to if he'd just acted like a grown man. Certainly not sitting four-deep in a Geo thinking about a diabolical Acadian fuck stick who'd been driven from New Orleans by the Feds.

It was maddening to contemplate, really, much of it easily avoidable, so I tried to go philosophical and take it all in stride. I failed at it, of course. I usually do.

The plan we worked up was to go down Delta by way of Rolling Fork, stop somewhere there, and make another plan. I offered to drop Luther out anywhere along the way since we weren't intending to travel down by Yazoo. Desmond was cutting south and west over toward 61.

"No sir," Luther told me, and he made noises like we were all kind of in this thing together. Who the hell would he be, he seemed to want to suggest, if he let his uncle face his trials alone.

It rang hollow, of course. There was the chance of swag at Eugene's, and Luther had a business stake in seeing us take the Acadian fuck stick down.

"I'll just ride on, if that's all right." He almost made it sound noble.

Desmond was drifting and whistling and distracted about some farming he'd done back in his skinny past, which is why he missed his turn and ended up driving all the way to Highway 1. That road runs north and south over by the

Mississippi, a part of the Delta that made me antsy even from the first.

Something got in my head about being backed against the river between the bridges up by Greenville and the one down Vicksburg way. I felt like cornered vermin anywhere west of Leland. If you found trouble back in those parts, you were well and royally stuck. About the only thing you could do was fight or drown.

Delta boys like Desmond, though, were used to being hemmed in. That was part of the general psyche of the place. So we rode down Highway 1, and I carried on like I was fine, but I was living for Desmond to cut back east, which he took his sweet time about. He finally turned at Grace and headed down past Otter Bayou to Lorenzen. Then he crossed the tracks and we came out hard by Rolling Fork.

Percy Dwayne remained indignant and pouty most of the way. He made the occasional pitiful noise about having his wife and his son snatched from him, accused me of worrying about nothing but a car.

He did his whole put-upon, victimized, it's-so-hard-to-be-a-white-guy thing that nobody with bat sense could possibly put an ounce of actual stock in. If he'd been black, he would have been rotting in Angola or Parchman for years already. Even cracker trash in the Delta got a better shake than Desmond and his ilk.

We stopped at the very service station where Percy Dwayne had met Eugene because Percy Dwayne had figured he could remember how to get to Eugene's from there. But Desmond and I together had soon noticed that something was off with Percy Dwayne. He wasn't acting like a man who was burning to get his wife and baby back. He didn't seem to have the drive you'd expect from a fellow in his shoes.

He went in the grocery mart after a soda and loitered for a while.

"What's up with him?" I asked Desmond, and together we put the question to Luther.

"Don't want to talk against him," Luther told us by way of preamble before acquainting me and Desmond with a raft of Percy Dwayne's failings as a Dubois, as a husband, as a man. "Could be Sissy just up and left him and ain't hoping to get found. Could be Percy Dwayne was telling damn lies all along."

"Then what's really up?" I asked him.

Luther shrugged. "Who the hell knows?"

"Tell me," I said to Luther, "about his wife."

He shrugged in a what's-to-tell sort of way. "He met her in Jackson. Some buddy of his threw them together. She comes from Vardamans over near Starkville."

"What do *you* think of her?"

Luther's face pinched up like he was smelling something unsavory. He shook his head a little. "She'll do any damn thing."

"Sort of girl to let herself get . . . kidnapped?"

"Can't figure why anybody'd want to take her. She'd cut your liver out if you gave her half a chance."

"What are you thinking?" Desmond asked me.

"The Ranchero needs saving," I told him. "Sissy and that baby? I'm not so sure about them."

"What difference does it make?" Luther wanted to know

"If the bullets start flying," I said, "I want to know who they're flying from."

"What bullets!?" Luther asked me.

"Won't come to that probably."

I glanced at Desmond for reassurance, but Desmond looked like a man persuaded that everything comes to a gunfight in the end.

FOURTEEN

Percy Dwayne finally came out of the grocery mart and joined us. He'd been reading the trading post. He'd found an El Camino fixer-upper near Belzoni. He'd torn the page out so he could show me the ad.

"That won't quite do," I told Percy Dwayne, who hadn't guessed it would.

"Where to?" Desmond asked him, but there were only a couple of choices. We could head south toward Vicksburg or east past Choctaw Landing in the direction of Holly Bluff.

Percy Dwayne directed us east through Delta wilderness, a whole nest of wildlife management areas. Scrubby, overgrown tax dodges for people too lazy to farm. Then we followed the road south toward the Delta National Forest—a primal, hellacious reminder of what the whole Delta used to be like. Before they'd cut down all the trees and plowed under all the thickets.

Once we got over to Holly Bluff and turned on the Spanish Fort road, Percy Dwayne couldn't quite recall how he'd gotten down to Eugene's.

"Sissy was driving," he told us, "and we were just following his truck. I know he's back in the woods somewhere. It'll hit me when I see it."

Desmond stopped and swallowed hard before he pulled into the national forest proper. There was just one road that bisected the place, and it was gravel and had snaky underbrush crowding it on either side.

"I know," I said to Desmond, "no bayous and no woods. I just want to thank you for doing this for me."

"I ain't done it yet," he told me, and we sat there for a while longer. But Desmond finally loosed a "Hmm" and gave the Geo gas.

The road followed some kind of pipeline. It was off in a ditch to one side. I can't say what might be getting pumped through the Delta National Forest. Could be sewage from Yazoo City, for all I knew, sent west to get sluiced into the mighty muddy. But that pipeline made for just the sort of landmark Percy Dwayne would be likely to recall.

"Yeah, yeah," he said. "That damn thing. The road'll bend up here, and you'll put that pipe behind you."

That's just what happened. The road turned right, and the pipeline kept straight through the scrub.

"It's up here on the left somewhere."

"What's it look like?" I asked Percy Dwayne.

"Hunting lodge, up on posts. We come out of the woods and there it was."

"Ain't no end of marijuana in this goddamn place," Luther piped in after having run silent for a while. "A man takes his life in his hands if he goes in there and thrashes around."

"I don't like the woods," Desmond announced. He seemed to need to hear himself say it.

As national forests go, this one wasn't easy to like. Bugs and bottomland. Scrub and hardwoods. Gators and vipers along with the biggest cypress trees I'd ever seen.

Luther wanted us to stop at every sign and pullout along the way. He seemed a little like a fellow on vacation.

"Don't you live around here?" I asked him.

He nodded and pointed nowhere much. "Didn't never hunt or nothing," he said. "Got no call to be in this place."

"You could come take a walk or something," I suggested, and Luther and Percy Dwayne (and Desmond a little, too) looked at me like I'd proposed they build a rocket and fly to Saturn. They were ready to ride an hour to get a loaf of bread but wouldn't have walked through the Delta National Forest without a blown head gasket or some sorry bastard making them do it with a gun.

I couldn't really blame them. It was about as gloomy a place as I've ever seen. Even though it was mid afternoon, the canopy was choking off the daylight, and everything seemed a little creepy there in the forest. We stopped to look at a sign planted along the road. It showed the way to a half-dozen camp sights off in the underbrush.

"Who'd camp in here?" I asked just generally to the wrong crowd altogether. They seemed to feel camping was like hiking only staggeringly worse.

We stopped so Luther could see a giant cypress tree up close. It was set off by a rail fence that circled it around. The trunk was about the diameter of a garage. Luther pulled out a pocket knife and plunged the blade in the trunk just because he could. For my part, I learned from an adjacent sign that the Delta National Forest was sixty-thousand acres of cypress trees and elms, sweetgums and giant nuttall oaks, not to mention the carpet of snake-rich underlay.

"It says here," I told Desmond and Luther and Percy Dwayne as well, "a Mississippi steam boat could burn thirty cords of wood a day." They all called me a damn liar, even Desmond, until they'd read it themselves.

We were stalling a little, I suspect, because once we started in with Eugene, that would put us onto Guy, and he promised to be genuine adult trouble. The meth lord career path tends to attract people you'd be better off leaving alone, and there we were on our way to bothering him but good. For a woman. For a baby. For a 1969 Ranchero. You could no more unbother a meth lord than unprovoke a cougar.

So we went slow and soaked in the peculiar attractions of the Delta National Forest. We stopped at trail heads and at a bayou full of turtles. We were all standing outside of the Geo peeing when Luther saw a bear. He thought it was a dog, then was sure it was a goat. Once it reached the road, Luther fell silent and climbed onto the roof of the car.

We finally came to a rough road off to the left four or five miles in. Percy Dwayne recognized it. Desmond pointed out the tire tracks in the mud. "Somebody back in here," Desmond said.

"Eugene's maybe a half mile back," Percy Dwayne told us. "Road gives out at the water."

It wasn't the sort of track that looked suitable for a Metro, so we left the car at the junction and got ready to walk in. I tried to take Desmond's mind off the deep, boggy woods that I'd personally dragged him into by giving him first dibs on our two-gun weapons cache.

Desmond selected Calvin's Steyr over K-Lo's shotgun. He said he didn't want to get in a firefight and find himself shooting rubber pellets. Desmond meant for anything he shot to go down and stay hit. Percy Dwayne insisted on getting armed, too, so I gave him the fireplace shovel. Luther was so fixed on his tap shoes—it seemed likely he'd get them muddy—that he didn't care if he was armed or not.

As we headed down that boggy tract, we weren't nearly as inconspicuous as we might have been. Luther leapt from rock to rock and *clack-clack*ed on every one while Percy Dwayne vented every little thing that popped into his head. Some of it was pertinent to the job at hand, but most of it was culinary. He'd gotten lunch twice at the Sonic, he told us, and still hadn't eaten shit.

Desmond would tell us "Hold on" every now again, and we'd stop so he could catch his breath.

"How much farther?" he kept asking Percy Dwayne, who kept being unable to say.

"You brought that Ranchero through here?" I asked him.

He nodded in a way that told me, "So fucking what if I did?"

About a half mile in we spotted the first deer. It was hanging upended from a sweet gum limb, neatly slit and bled.

"Eugene?" Desmond asked Percy Dwayne.

He nodded. "Half the tamales all over this place got his venison in them."

I heard the first dog along about then, and it didn't sound like a hound. More like the kind of dog you'd have if you lived out on a bayou and didn't want anybody messing with your shit.

"Did you see his dogs?" I asked Percy Dwayne.

"Only heard them," he told me.

"How many?"

"Wouldn't worry about them. They was shut up in a pen out back."

The road opened up about fifty yards before us. The sunlight managed to find it, anyway, and I could make out the hint of a roofline through the trees off to the left—the only purely straight thing anywhere.

"Does Eugene have a wife or kids? Anybody else up there?"

"Not fit for people," Luther said, which was a hell of a

thing coming from him. "He's got running buddies. Cousins and such. Some of them might be around."

"He took you to Guy or Guy came to you?"

"Come to us," Percy Dwayne told me.

"Eugene called him?"

Percy Dwayne nodded.

"How long before he got here?"

"Half an hour at the most."

"So he's around here somewhere, too."

"Maybe. Somewhere. There's an awful lot of here to go around."

That was just the sort of sentiment to register with Desmond, and he must have felt the great swarming weight of the wilderness upon him because he stopped where he was. He peered all around. He swallowed hard and uncorked a doleful "Hmmm."

"What?" I asked him.

"Promise me something," Desmond said.

I nodded that I would.

"Whatever happens," he told me, "swear you won't leave me here."

FIFTEEN

Percy Dwayne and Luther together identified Eugene's truck, which we could see a little of in the clearing up ahead. It was a Ford/Chevy/International hybrid that somebody with middling welding skills had slapped together and fitted up. It was the sort of thing the Clampetts would have driven to Beverly Hills if they had been a little less fussy and safety conscious.

The bed was loaded with chairs, wooden folding ones. It turned out Eugene had spirited them away from a Moose Lodge across the river, over in Lake Providence. He'd been hauling them around the day before and had boasted about them to Percy Dwayne. Eugene had come to believe that if he crossed the river into Arkansas and stole something over there, they couldn't arrest him for it once he'd brought it back to Mississippi.

"I sure don't want to get shot," Desmond said, "by somebody as stupid as that."

We worked our way on up the road until the scrub thinned out and the thicket gave way where Eugene had been fighting it a little. I can't really say why he'd bothered given the calamitous state of his yard. The truck he drove was parked at the edge of it, flanked by the trucks he'd made it from. Then there were lumpy bits of other things that the grass and the sticker vines had taken. Cast-off appliances, tractor parts, a couple of leaky johnboats—all of it swallowed up with thickety weeds and ornamented with garbage. It looked like nearly every thorn in the yard had snagged a shopping bag.

We could hear someone talking. Two people, it turned out, having an argument. They were yelling at each from over toward the house, which was stirring up the dogs. They were yelping and barking and snarling in what I hoped was a sturdy pen.

"Eugene?" I asked Percy Dwayne.

He listened close, and when one of those men held forth about what a jackass the other one was, Percy Dwayne told me, "That one's him."

"What about the other one? Guy?" I said hopefully.

Percy Dwayne just shook his head and shrugged.

It was difficult to figure a good way to go at Eugene's house. The building was up on stilts, and there was just one set of steps leading to the deck. We could see underneath clear out to the water, which turned out to be a section of the Little Sunflower River. It was a slow, swampy passage, a half-stagnant bayou. The shallow eddies under the house were full of beer cans and trash.

The only way in was up the steps, and Eugene might well hear us coming. Everything looked set to give and waver once you put your weight upon it. I wasn't quite sure but that Desmond might bring the whole place down.

Eugene and his buddy were arguing, it turned out, about catfish they'd caught. Not so much the weight and size but what they'd caught them with. Eugene's buddy had some kind of spinning lure with holy properties, while Eugene had a plug he swore by, which he smeared all over with Baitmate. They went on at heated profane length about who'd caught more with what.

As we stood there figuring what to do, beer cans started hitting the water. The more they argued about their catfish lures, the quicker they seemed to drink.

"All right," I said, "let's try this. You," I told Percy Dwayne, "go up there and knock on the door. Tell Eugene and his buddy you're coming with Guy's money."

"Why am I bringing Guy's money to him?"

"Because you can't find Guy, and you've come out here to see if Eugene'll help you."

"I wouldn't come out here with money. He'd knock me on the head and take it."

"Then what do you want to tell him?"

"I want to ask him for a beer. Tell him I'm lost or something."

"He'll go for that?" I asked him.

Percy Dwayne nodded and spat.

"Well, go on, then," I said. "We'll be under here." I pointed to a moderately swampy spot beneath the decking. "You get him down those steps any way you can."

Eugene and his buddy had worked each other into twin dudgeons by then. They might have started out with catfish lures, but they'd progressed to larger matters. I couldn't tell who was who at the time, but the one with the phlegmier hack was informing the stutterer he knew precisely fuck all and so wasn't just a fishing lure ignoramus but made do as an all-purpose tool.

The one with the stutter took exception. He was convinced he had talents and skills far in excess of anything the phlegmy one could hope for.

Because they were swamp rats, they got down to dicks and women straightaway. Most men—particularly your suburban two-cars-and-a-mower sort—would have descended in stages from fishing lures to mechanical aptitude to sporting ability to alcohol tolerance to women and manly equipment. These fellows went straight from catfish lures to gals they'd pleased and how.

They had in common a woman named Ailene and some creature named Dotty, and they started trading descriptions of just how they'd gone at these girls. It would have qualified as clinical if they'd known between them anything about female anatomy. That exchange was hard to tolerate in the muck under Eugene's nasty house.

Even Percy Dwayne stopped halfway up the stairs and gave us a pleading look. He didn't appear so much leery and fearful as disgusted. The phlegmy one had a particular way with bodily descriptions in that everything came out sounding like science fiction. All the parts he'd seen and touched and licked and probed with his mighty saber could have passed in the telling for bits of a lizard warrior from Alpha Centauri.

The stutterer was more of a romantic in that he only strangled his girls a little. He went on at some length about Dotty, who, apparently, was livestock-sized and lived her whole life in front of her television. He claimed to have gotten a rise out of her, some sort of orgasmic discharge that the phlegmy one told him emphatically was a goddamn lie.

That's about when they stopped chatting and started grunting and swearing instead.

Percy Dwayne had gained the landing by then and was loitering just above us. He looked down at us over the decking rail and shook his head. Whatever was going on between those fellows was nothing he wanted to walk into. I pointed K-Lo's shotgun at him to help him along.

So Percy Dwayne decided to ease around at least a little. Eugene and his buddy by then didn't even have the breath for swearing but were chiefly wheezing instead.

"Tussling?" I asked.

Luther and Desmond suspected I was right.

Luther buffed his shoe tops on his trousers and added, "Wouldn't want them to kill each other."

"Right," I told him. "Go up there and help your uncle out."

"I ain't like him," Luther told us as if we were Delta Muskateers. "I could have gone home."

"But you didn't," Desmond told him and showed him the barrel of that Steyr. "Go give Percy Dwayne a push."

Luther marched up the stairs all *clickety-clack*ing. He shoved Percy Dwayne before him and said, "Go on."

They rounded the corner and must have slipped up on Eugene and his buddy who had every right not to expect a drop-in visit where they were.

"Hey here." It was Percy Dwayne.

The next thing we heard was the deck rail cracking. A length of it smacked the water behind us, and me and Desmond had just turned at the sound when Eugene and his buddy hit the bayou all tangled up together.

"Gone over," Luther shouted.

"We see it," I told him.

The fall stunned them both, one worse than the other. They were filthy, whiskery coots, looked like a pair of water-logged muskrats, and one of them was flapping his arms and sputtering while the other was floating facedown.

"Well, shit," I said as I handed my gun to Desmond and waded out in the swampy water. It was warm and silty and trash strewn. I kept waiting to step on an alligator. The alternative was about two feet of mud.

"Turn him over," I yelled to the sputtering swamp rat, but his eyes were big, and he just flapped his arms and snorted. He wasn't in danger of drowning. The water where he stood was only waist-deep.

"Eugene?" I asked him, and he pointed at the guy face-down beside him. I felt at that moment put upon and pathetic like a proper Delta cracker. Wouldn't you know the shiftless bastard we had authentic use for would be the one in the bayou about to drown.

"Help him," I suggested, and the fellow with the wide eyes and the flapping arms told me I could g-g-go f-f-fuck myself.

Once I got close to him, I glanced up at Luther and Percy Dwayne on the deck. "They just fell," Percy Dwayne said, and pointed. "That one there's Eugene."

"Got it," I said, and looked back down in time to see Eugene's buddy pull a pistol out of his pants and point it at me.

It was a soaking wet .22 buntline, a revolver with the barrel sawn off. It had live rounds in the chambers. I could see them plain enough.

"I don't know you," he told me.

"He's going to drown."

"So?" he said.

"Isn't he a buddy of yours?"

"Don't know that he is," he said.

"Well, today he's a buddy of mine. Let's you and me roll him over."

I took a couple of steps toward him, was almost within arm's reach. He drew the hammer back with a soggy click.

"Hold on here," he told me.

Dry-land trash is bad enough. But they go out in the world with people as a regular sort of thing, so they can behave like they're domesticated whenever they see fit. Swamp trash is something else altogether. They tend to feed themselves from what they catch and shoot, rarely get past the nearest grocery mart and service station unless they need hardware they can't manufacture or have had an appendix explode.

They're suspicious of everybody who's not swamp trash like them, and they'd just as soon sink you in the bayou and let the gators at you than run the risk of getting lied to and beguiled by you.

"You the law, ain't you?"

"No."

Percy Dwayne called down helpfully, "He ain't no goddamn body."

"Then what the shit you doing out here?"

It was all a little too Socratic for my taste at the moment. I managed to grab Eugene by the leg of his overalls. His pal didn't like that much and poked my kidney with his pistol, which put his face about where I needed it to be to break his nose.

I shot an elbow back his way, quick and brutal like a piston. I caught him flush on the bridge but maybe a little harder than I'd meant to. It was his own fault. He was making stupid trouble where trouble didn't need to be.

He managed a groan and pitched over backwards. His

pistol went flying out into the swamp, and he sank beneath the surface in a mix of blood and bubbles.

I turned Eugene over, shook him hard, and he brought up a quart of bayou. I had to drag him by the collar over to Desmond who was perched upon a hummocky clump of weeds beneath the house. He yanked Eugene clear of the water and dropped him onto the ground which knocked another dose of bayou from him and probably a couple of Milwaukee's Bests.

"What about him?" Desmond asked me, and pointed with his forehead to the other fellow still out in the swamp. The only thing breaking the surface was the toe of his right boot.

I moaned and turned to wade back out. That boy was a bloody mess. His nose was flowing, and he might have thought he was sputtering before, but he was truly sputtering now. He was deeply indignant, of course, and wanted to tell me all about the world of hurt him and all his slack-ass swamp-rat relations were going to put on me.

What with the blood and the swallowed water and all the heated stuttering, there was an awful lot of gruesome splatter attached to the whole ordeal. I paused before handing him over to Desmond so I could advise him, "Shut up!"

We laid the two of them out on the ground at the bottom of the stairs, and once they came to their regular senses, they started arguing all over again. Eugene was persuaded his buddy, Tommy, had shoved him through the railing. Tommy didn't remember it that way at all.

"I can tell you this," Eugene said at last, "you don't know

shit about Dotty." And with that, they started tussling all afresh.

There was yelling and blood and biting and swearing and rolling around on the muddy ground. Luther and Percy Dwayne watched it all from high on the landing while me and Desmond stood there and watched them from up close.

"And here I thought the day might come," Desmond told me, "when I'd understand white people."

SIXTEEN

Eugene's house was about the damnedest thing I'd ever seen.
It was all Li'l Abner—put together as providence allowed.
To judge by the evidence, Eugene had built a platform and
slapped a dwelling on top of it. Then he had added and de-
molished and tweaked and rearranged, depending on what
he'd stolen or found or maybe even bought outright.

There was one whole room where the outer wall was made
entirely from doors, and Eugene had popped a few panels
here and there to caulk in glass for windows. He had siding
made from rusty sheeting off some kind of grain bin and roof
shingles that were road signs upended and nailed down. He'd
made lavish use of tar paper and tin flashing, and he had a

chimney pipe that was a culvert he'd probably pulled out of somebody's driveway. He'd fashioned a deckside toilet out of a plastic water tank. Everything went straight down into the bayou, which filled me with desperation for a tetanus shot.

Tommy's nose bled for longer than was interesting or convenient. We finally ended up packing his nostrils with balled-up pages from a Cabela's catalog just so he'd shut up about the leakage.

For people as filthy as those two, they were confoundingly particular about their clammy clothes. That dunk in the bayou was probably the first time they'd been wet in a couple of weeks, and all they could do was complain about the mud and the blood and the swamp stink. Before we knew it, they'd both stripped down to their filthy underwear. Then they shed their briefs and stood around complaining naked.

Eugene had a thing or two to say to Percy Dwayne about all the trouble Percy Dwayne had caused him. It seemed Eugene hadn't gotten much peace at all since they'd run up on each other at the gas mart. Guy was all over him to work on his car and haul stuff for him and shit.

"What car?"

"That damn pink thing," Eugene told me.

"What kind of work?"

"Pipes and paint mostly. A little carburetor tweaking."

"Done any of it?"

"What the hell do you care?"

"It's kind of his car," Percy Dwayne said.

"Not no more," Eugene told me, "unless you want to be fucking with Guy. And ain't nobody nowhere wants to be fucking with Guy."

"He'll kill your ass," Tommy said. Then he cackled so enthusiastically he shot a bloody catalog page from his nose.

"Tell me about him," I said to Eugene.

"Can't he put some damn clothes on first?" Luther had endured all he could stand of nasty, naked swamp rats.

We all stepped inside Eugene's house proper, and Luther yanked a blanket off the couch to give to Tommy so he could cover himself up. It turned out to be the only thing holding the stuffing and the ossified mouse shit in. A cloud of dust boiled up, all desiccation and dander. We threw open what doors we could find, and Desmond punched a Desmond-sized hole in a width of tar paper siding that was the only thing between Eugene's sitting room and the great outdoors.

"That's right," Eugene told us all, "tear it up." Then he went and got wounded and pouty, and him and Percy Dwayne bonded over how plagued and put upon they were.

"Where does Guy live?" I asked Eugene.

"Who the fuck wants to know?"

Weary now, I raised the shotgun barrel toward the ceiling, more or less aimed it at an orange and black MOWING AHEAD sign, and squeezed off a shell without really thinking just what I was up to.

Lead pellets would have punched on through, and we'd have been left with just some instructive racket, but the little rubber balls I was shooting stayed in the house and went everywhere fast. They hit that sign and came back down, bounced all over the place. They filled that room just like a swarm of hornets.

Those pellets hurt so much through my clothes I was doubly glad I wasn't standing around naked. Tommy, for his part, balled up on the couch and ducked under his filthy blanket while Eugene couldn't think of a thing to do but wail and leap and dance.

"What the hell did you do that for?" Luther wanted to know.

"Crazy son-of-a-bitch," Percy Dwayne added.

Tommy came out from under his blanket to add a few choice words as well. Eugene just whined and flopped around on the floor.

Like most rash things I get up to, that one hadn't been helpful.

Even Desmond, after a great while, told me, "Let's don't be doing that again."

It did have the effect of prompting Eugene to pack his jewels away and put on some clothes. While he dressed, I took occasion to soak in his décor. One part tumbledown furniture and one part dusty taxidermy. He had stuffed deer heads and stuffed racoons, a stuffed carp, a lacquered rattler, a couple of dusty armadillos, a mangy bear cub, and way up high on top of a cabinet a spotted stuffed bobcat. It was perched on a rock, ready to pounce, with its red lacquered tongue sticking out.

"Hey," I said to Desmond, and pointed.

"I'll be damned."

I opened the cabinet doors, used a shelf for a step, climbed up, and fetched it down.

"Where did you get this?" I asked Eugene.

"Aw, hell," he told me, and started in with a fanciful spot of rubbish about how he'd run up on it down bayou a bit while he was out one morning baiting trot lines.

"He was downwind," he told me. "Had the sun behind him. He was setting up an awful fuss."

As soon as I'd opened the cabinet door to climb up and fetch the thing down, Luther had taken the exposed contents as an invitation to plunder. That cupboard was crammed full of other people's mail, a couple of rusty old pistols, a few rifle parts, and one school-bus yellow Taser that caught Luther's eye.

"I've always wanted one of these," he said. "It's like having a super power."

By then Eugene was describing how he'd eased down in a slot where he could get off a shot at his bobcat. Luther, for his part, was turning that Taser around his hands trying to figure how to fire it up.

"Think it works?" he wanted to know.

I took it from him. "Let's see." I switched it on. It charged right up. I fired a dart into Eugene's shoulder just as he was about to bring his bobcat down.

The element of surprise coupled with fifteen hundred volts put Eugene off his story all at once.

"Try again," I told him, and then pointed at K-Lo's stuffed

bobcat and pulled the trigger to give Eugene a little electric incentive.

"Got it from a boy." He was shouting by now. "Some gang-banging nigger up in Greenville. Take it," Eugene told me. "Go on. I don't care."

"Works fine," I told Luther.

"Can I have it?"

"I don't see why not."

There were a dozen tactical reasons against lingering at Eugene's, in addition to the fact that Desmond couldn't tolerate a filthy house with a lacquered snake inside. Desmond motioned for me to join him on the deck so he could tell me as much.

"All right," I said. "So what do we do?"

It was nearly dark by then. The frogs were starting up out in the bayou, and the mosquitoes were fairly swarming.

"We'll head up north. Take them with us. They can lead us to Guy tomorrow."

"Take them how?"

And we both stood there studying Eugene's welded, jack-leg truck.

It drove pretty well for a vehicle made by a swamp rat with marginal skills. The drive shaft knocked, and it drifted if you let it, but that truck got up the road well enough for a slap-dash piece of junk.

I was following Desmond. He was riding alone in his Geo, which I'd arranged as a courtesy to him. I had Luther and Percy Dwayne up front with me and Eugene and Tommy in the bed. They were under a tarp and taped up snug because they'd assured me there wasn't a fellow on earth who could take them any damn where.

"Tell me about Guy," I charged Percy Dwayne.

He went agonized on me and started in with Sissy and little PD, but I had a question for him about them as well. "What in the name of hell," I asked him, "would he want with your wife and son?"

Luther piled on. He had Sissy issues and general toddler misgivings, so he also was anxious to hear what sort of ruthless meth lord bastard would snatch a woman and her baby and keep them kidnapped in his house.

"What's he need the headache for? He can buy any woman he wants."

Percy Dwayne just snorted and groaned, couldn't find the truth at first. That's the Dubois way. When you've been bred and raised to connive, the facts never feel quite right in your mouth. There's no finagling or fabrication to the honest gospel truth, no angles to work, no details to plant, no foreseeable payoff. That made being square tough for Percy Dwayne because he wasn't remotely a truth-is-its-own-reward sort of guy.

But a kidnapped wife and toddler didn't make enough sense to swallow, so we teased it out of him a little at a time. It turned out he and the wife had been butting heads for a month or two by then. As a Vardaman, Sissy came from a pack of ambitious, cold-blooded felons, the sort of people who adjusted their lawlessness and thuggery to the times. She couldn't see that sort of flexibility or drive in Percy Dwayne. He'd started out as a thief and a chisler and had stayed one ever since.

"Always on me about gumption and how I don't have enough," he said. "Then she met Guy. He's fucking gumptioned to the gills."

"I hear he looks like some kind of movie star," Luther added, burying the shiv.

Percy Dwayne told him. "He ain't all that much."

Luther shook his head and spat out the window. "You're just a nickel and dimer. All you've ever been."

"Listen to you," Percy Dwayne said, disgusted.

"I'm entrepreneurial," Luther informed him.

"Sitting in a bar all day selling pills and shit?"

"I've got clients," Luther said as he smoothed out a lapel. "I'm building relationships. What the hell have you got?"

"I don't see how slinging dope is better than what I do."

"I don't even know what the fuck you do," Luther told him.

"So did he take them or not?" I asked Percy Dwayne.

Percy Dwayne didn't say anything for about a half a minute. Then he shook his head and mumbled, "I don't know."

"You don't know?"

"They was there and then they weren't."

"And all that shit with Calvin?"

"Just trying to get me some . . ." Percy Dwayne trailed off.

"Gumption?" I said.

"I guess."

"So the Acadian fuck stick picked you clean?"

Percy Dwayne dropped his head and nodded. "I'm going to get her back," he told us, "one way or another."

Once we'd reached Indianola, Desmond shot straight over the truck route and went up to check on his momma. I pulled in behind the KFC and parked beside the dumpster. It was half past eight by then, and K-Lo had been closed for an hour and a half. I figured, if I was lucky, he might be only about half drunk.

I fished that bobcat out of the back of the trunk and checked on Eugene and Tommy. They'd been bounced around enough by then to have altered their attitudes. I took the tape off Eugene's mouth long enough for him to tell me that they were ready to be decent and ride up front in the cab. The mercury lights at the KFC made him think we were in Jackson, and Eugene got frantic just being out of the woods and away from the swamp.

He started yelling. Not for help, but more in the way a wild pig might squeal. It was as if, in his puny swamp-rat brain, he couldn't think what else to do. So I retaped him, pulled the tarp back over them both, and tied it off.

I went to the front door of the rental store so K-Lo could see me come up. I looked for him on the ugly sofa, but he didn't appear to be about. I peered in through the glass doors, and when I couldn't find him, I knocked. He came out of the back with his little plastic lunch container in hand, the one he brought in every morning full of rice and eggplant and chicken and carried home rinsed out every night.

K-Lo unlocked the door and pushed it open. I was planning on going in, but he came out and bolted the thing behind him.

"Where are you going?" I asked him.

"Home," he said. "I can't sit around here. I'm still shook up about last night."

"You're not even drunk," I told him.

"I'm drunk a little," he said, "but I don't want to die in this place on that ugly sofa."

"So you're just locking up and going on home?"

K-Lo nodded.

"Good for you," I told him. "Why don't you take this with you."

I stepped clear of the bobcat, which had been sitting behind me on the sidewalk all the while.

K-Lo gasped. He flat sucked air. He reminded me of those people who used to show up on TV and get reunited with long-lost siblings, old army buddies, former loves. They'd gasp like that. It was a way of saying with just air and spasm, "For the love of Christ, I thought you were dead."

K-Lo didn't move at first, appeared as if he couldn't, as if the sight of his bobcat had to be some sort of galling mirage.

He said, "But . . ." a time or two while he stayed just where he was. I picked that cat up to prove it was real and put it in his hands.

I was sure for a second there Kalil the hothead was going

to up and cry, and not the usual tears of bitterness and disappointment, but genuine tears of joy and of relief. He didn't,
though. He remembered himself.

"Did I ever tell you how I killed him?"

I shook my head. I told him, "Not that I recall."

"I was driving home one night, almost to Leland. I seem
to recall I hit him with my car."

"Never heard you recall that part before."

K-Lo shrugged. "Where did you find him?"

"Down Delta. A fellow had bought him somewhere.
Gave him to me when I said it was yours."

"Tell him I'm glad to have him back."

"I'll do that. Don't leave him here. Somebody'll just snatch
him again."

K-Lo nodded. K-Lo said, "All right."

I watched as K-Lo loaded his bobcat in the backseat of
his Honda. Then he pulled out on the truck route, margin-
ally sober, and drove home to his wife and son.

I bought two buckets of chicken from a pimply kid at the
KFC counter who appeared to have taken his corporate train-
ing to heart. He was polite and efficient, must have been new
on the job. Everybody else in the place—the employees and
the diners—looked to be wading through honey to get wher-
ever they went.

Pearl intercepted us in the driveway, halfway to the car
shed. She'd already eaten her supper, but she put on like she
hadn't. Luther made a fuss over her and introduced her to

his uncle. Eugene and Tommy were more of a problem since their hands were taped behind their backs. They were properly dressed by now and not conspicuously nasty, but Tommy still had catalog pages up his nose.

"Say hello to Mrs. Jarvis," I told them.

"Pearl," she said, and invited the whole pack of us in.

She didn't appear to let herself see that Tommy and Eugene were restrained. Pearl had a talent for selective obliviousness. It always applied to family, especially her worthless son, who Pearl could construe as loving and attentive, but she could extend it when she wanted to the rest of the world as well.

"I see you've got chicken," Pearl said. It's hard to miss those red and white buckets. "Come on in. I've got a big table we can all sit around and a bowl of potato salad I made this morning."

I thought of Pearl's mayonnaise that had gone more yellow than beige. I wondered if Rusty was dead.

Pearl and Luther and Percy Dwayne went on into the house while I lingered on the back porch with Tommy and Eugene.

"Where the hell is this?" Tommy wanted to know.

"Still Mississippi," I told him. "I'll cut you loose if you can behave."

"I'm fucking starving," Eugene said.

"Mouth," I told him. "You treat that woman like your mother."

Come to find out Tommy and Eugene never had much use for their mothers, and worse still, Eugene announced he'd like to turn Pearl upside down. Then him and Tommy started in on who had the tool and the prowess to make Pearl squeal like Dotty and Ailene.

I didn't know what else to do but smack them each one time, which they curled their lips and got all peevish about.

"You've seen people on TV, right, people with table manners?"

They nodded. Each had a hand to ear I'd cuffed him on.

"Act like them for the next little while, and you'll be all right. Otherwise I'm turning Luther loose with the Taser."

The hell of it was, they were perfectly stellar company in the house. It was partly the threat of getting electrocuted, but it was mostly Pearl's way of treating everybody the same. I can't say how she came by it since it's hardly the Southern way. Class lines down in Dixie rival those of the British peerage, but Pearl just didn't see the world that way. She wanted company, so she made allowances, saw in people what she wanted to see, and her approach had a way of making guests more than they should have been.

Once Pearl had gotten out the silver and the tatted linen place mats, the crystal water glasses even though they were cracked and chipped, once she charged Tommy and Percy Dwayne to bring the china out, nobody was a lowlife or a swamp rat anymore.

Pearl put the chicken on a platter, brought out the poison potato salad, and chirped that we should all join hands for grace. Eugene, of all people, volunteered to say a prayer he knew, and he was going on about the Savior in heroic couplets when I peeked around the table like I had the night before.

"God help me," I prayed to myself in silence, "if this gets ordinary."

SEVENTEEN

"Gentle giant," Pearl told me.

I was in the kitchen drying the dishes by then, and she'd been asking after Desmond, who Pearl had taken a real shine to.

"I like a man who's neat," she said. "Gil was neat."

"I'm hoping," I said to Pearl, "I'll have Gil's car back by tomorrow."

"I know you'll do what you can," she told me. I'm sure that would have been enough for her whether it produced a Ranchero or not. The trouble for me was that doing and failing wouldn't have been sufficient.

Then I got lost in a reverie over what I might meet with in Guy, since I'd come across lots of Delta trash since I'd moved to Mississippi. A ruthless Acadian fuck stick in charge of a genuine criminal concern was not the sort to rent a TV and have it reclaimed on him. I had to think Guy was entirely his own type of thing.

While I was standing drying dishes and ruminating, I lost track of my charges. I suddenly realized I couldn't hear them in the dining room anymore. I asked Pearl if she knew where they'd gone.

She led me back to her guest room where they were all deep in Gil's closet. Eugene was wearing a navy blue double-breasted blazer over his bib overalls. He didn't look transformed exactly, but the swamp rat was largely submerged. Even Tommy, who'd found one of Gil's impeccably clean jump suits, could have passed for a suburban husband with a Chevrolet to tinker on and lawn fertilizer to spread. Percy Dwayne had found a suit coat and, just like his nephew Luther, he looked like a minor Chicago thug from eighty years ago.

"You mind?" I asked Pearl.

"Lord no," she told me. "Somebody should get use of those clothes."

"How did he end up with so many?" Luther asked her.

She fingered Luther's lapel with a sad, distracted smile. "I'd buy them. I doubt he ever put half of them on."

On the way back to the kitchen, Pearl remembered a charge she'd been given. "That policeman came by," she told me, and tapped her head. "The one with the bandage. He doubts you're in Texas. Wanted me to give you this."

Dale had written me a note on the back of a traffic ticket. He had the penmanship of a middle schooler. "The longer you hide," he'd written, "the worse it'll be."

"I don't care for him," Pearl confided. "He's got those beady eyes."

I marked Dale down as one of the few humans Pearl wouldn't give a sports coat to.

We bid Pearl good night and marched up the steps to my place over the car shed. I turned on my TV, and Tommy and Eugene sat down on my ratty settee. I tossed them the remote, and they went sailing through the channels all but hypnotized. It was like I'd given them a double dose of Benadryl, and I couldn't help but think they'd be content there for a while.

"I'm going to go check on Desmond," I told Luther and Percy Dwayne. "I need him," I said of Eugene, "for tomorrow. It'd be a good thing to find him here when I get back."

"I hear you, Chief," Luther told me. He reached into his jacket pocket and brought out his school-bus yellow Taser.

"There's beer in the fridge. Chips in the cabinet. I won't be long."

I went out the door and down the steps. I skulked around the yard for a bit, in the shadows out of reach of the vapor lights. There wasn't a thing parked on the street but Eugene's claptrap truck. I jogged down to it, climbed in, and drove away in a cloud of incinerated engine oil.

I got up to Sunflower before I stopped for gas. I was going to do Eugene a favor by filling up his tank, but I kept pumping and pumping and the damn thing wouldn't finish. It turned out he had four or five gas tanks daisy-chained together. Filling that truck was like trying to fuel a passenger jet. I quit once I'd closed on sixty dollars, the far end of what my Visa would currently allow.

I drove past Desmond's on 49 and then cut back down at Blaine. It didn't seem sensible that Dale would be sitting on Desmond instead of me, but Dale wasn't the sensible sort. I scoped out Desmond's place up and back since Dale wouldn't know the truck, and I finally pulled in once I was satisfied nobody was about.

I went around to the back door, and Desmond let me in. I could smell the Oxy as soon as I stepped inside.

"Momma had a bad day," Desmond told me.

"Has a doctor seen her lately?"

Desmond shook his head the way people do in the Delta when, instead of "No," they mean, "How am I going to pay for that?"

I went back to say hello to Desmond's mother and walked into a thing I'd never expected to see. She was in the bed, under the covers from about the waist down. She was wearing a flannel house dress with daffodils all over it, and her wig was sitting pretty nearly straight upon her head.

She had one of the pills I'd bought from Luther on a square of Reynolds Wrap, a little piece about the size of an unfolded chewing gum wrapper. She held a lighter underneath and heated that pill until it was smoking and melting. Then she inhaled the vapor through a little piece of drinking straw.

It was the sort of thing you'd see every day on the out-skirts of Lauderdale, where the storefront doctors write script for Oxy junkies, but in an old black lady's bedroom in rural Mississippi? I'd thought she'd just break those pills into pieces, swallow one, and go to sleep. This felt a hell of a lot more desperate than that would have.

"Hey," I said. "How we feeling?"

"No good," she told me, and took another hit.

Then she set her works on the nightstand and lay back against the headboard. I watched her for a little while and then went back to the kitchen.

"How'd she get started on that stuff?" I asked Desmond, which was exactly the wrong thing to ask him because he was the one who'd gotten her going when her regular pain meds had run out.

"Right after Shawnica, I was in a bad way. Couldn't take life straight anymore. Never had much stomach for liquor, but the Oxy worked all right."

"How'd you get off?"

Desmond gave that one some thought. The easy answer was he got sick of bouncing along the bottom, but it's always a little more complicated than that.

"You get fed up with nine-to-five, you start doing drugs. You get fed up with drug life, you go back to nine-to-five."

"Did getting stabbed by Luther fit in there somewhere?"

"Maybe," Desmond told me. "A little."

"We've got to get your mother to a doctor somehow be-fore she burns the goddamn house down."

Desmond nodded, but he was just humoring me now.

We walked out the back door and into the yard. It was one of those beautiful Delta nights, but for the mosquitoes. Stars from horizon to horizon, just a smudge of light from Indianola down south.

"How are the swamp boys?" Desmond asked me.

"Watching *SportsCenter*. Seemed happy enough. Pearl's got them all in jackets."

Desmond laughed his muffled snort like a sneeze from the end of a pipe.

"What time tomorrow?" he asked me.

I shrugged. "Up and out early, I guess. You know you don't have to come. I can probably handle Guy."

"I'll be there," Desmond told me.

"I'll get that Ranchero tomorrow or quit trying. Damned if I've ever gone to such fuss for a car."

We walked around toward the front of the house where I'd parked Eugene's truck.

"How's that thing drive?" he asked me.

"Better than you'd think, but it gets the mileage of a motor grader." I climbed up and in. "Take care of your mother," I told Desmond.

"Can't do nothing else."

I drove down the Dwyer Road to Sunflower along the railroad track. There was moonlight shining on the cornstalks, across the soybeans and the wheat. The few houses I passed were still and unlit. I didn't meet any traffic. The Delta at night can be like a trash pile under a few inches of fresh snow—beauty alone untouched by squalor and unleavened with desperation. I took my time driving back to Pearl's and enjoyed myself a little too much.

What I mean to say is, I got sloppy. It's hard to be looking out all the time, particularly when you know you're being dogged by a troglodyte like Dale. When I didn't see his cruiser on the street in front of Pearl's, I just parked the truck with two wheels in the ditch and headed for the driveway.

I was ten yards up it when Dale came out from behind a camellia bush. He was wearing a bandage on his head that looked like a sanitary napkin, and he was in street clothes, which for Dale meant a velour track suit. This one was maroon with navy piping, and it made Dale look out of place there in the middle of Pearl's driveway. He would have been more at home in the Short Hills Mall or an Olive Garden anywhere.

"Texas my ass," Dale said.

"Hey, Dale," I told him.

"Where's your shovel, little man?"

I showed him my empty hands.

Dale had a sap in his waistband. He pulled it out and waved it at me, tossed it into the yard.

"Just me and you. Let's see who goes down now."

By then I was actively sifting through my options. High on my list was running down the street as fast as I could manage. The track suit notwithstanding, Dale was anything but fleet. I'd seen where the sap landed, and that was a possibility, but what if I hit him with it, and it only made him madder? A sap's all right, but it's not in the league with a Dubois fireplace shovel.

Dale was hoping for a fight. He was so juiced and built that I had to doubt a human fist could hurt him. There was a small chance he had a glass jaw and I could put him down, but I didn't want to get taken apart trying to find it out.

So I was looking for a tool, anything stout I could poke or pummel him with. There was a cement deer in the neighbor's yard, but I doubted I could pick it up. I glanced down the road the other way. Just garbage cans and recycling bins.

I knew he wouldn't be much of a puncher. Dale was too musclebound for that. But that didn't mean he couldn't crush me into a powder, and I found myself actively trying to calculate which hospital was closest—in case I needed something set or sewn.

Dale began dancing on his toes and telling me, "Let's get it on!" I flashed on Dale and Patty, perched together on their sofa, watching far too much Spike TV.

"Right," I said. "Let's do that."

I figured on being all elbows. I'd break his nose like Tommy's. I'd try to catch him in the throat, kick him in his shriveled testicles if it came to that. I would have preferred to pull a thorn from his paw, but that didn't seem to be an option.

So I went through all the usual prep for getting myself beat up, was trying to get psychologically set for the pain, but Dale kept distracting me. He was the sort who had to talk his way into a fight.

Dale felt compelled to tell me about my upcoming destruction, the hurt he'd rain down on me, the blood he'd cause
to flow. I watched him shadowbox in a bid to loosen up his
veiny arms and listened to him talk about pieces of me he
meant to pulverize. The effect was more in the way of bore-
dom than intimidation.

I was five seconds away from just bum rushing the guy. I
figured I might as well fly all over him and see what that ac-
complished, and I was cocked and poised and primed to spring
when Dale began to jiggle and drool. I thought the steroids
had finally gotten to him and he was having some kind of
stroke or that maybe there was such a thing as a too-dumb-
to-live seizure.

He stayed on his feet and just wiggled around, all spastic
and galvanic, until he finally toppled over on Pearl's cement
drive and broke his fall with his forehead. Only then did I see
Luther, who'd been eclipsed by Dale's bulk. He was standing
there on the driveway with his yellow Taser in hand, attached
to Dale by the darts in his back and the wires that ran out of
them.

Luther had caught Dale in the trapezius, a slightly left of
center shot. He gave a recreational pull on the Taser trigger
just to see Dale flop a little on the drive.

"Never did much care for baseball," Luther told me.

"He's bleeding," I said.

It was worse than that really. Dale was sluicing blood onto
the driveway. Dale groaned and rolled around enough to earn
another jolt.

"We ought to take him somewhere," Luther said, and I was picturing some pullout on the roadside, but Luther had the emergency room over in Greenville in mind. So we wrestled him into the back of the truck and drove him west toward the river. We set Dale off by a dumpster where they threw out medical waste. Then Luther went in and made out like he'd just strayed across him and some other shiftless sorts had dropped him off.

"Bad cut," Luther told me once we'd got back on the truck route. "I think I saw his skull."

"He's a tough one," I said. "Dale'll be all right."

You would have thought the previous two days would have taught me how fragile people are, how things can be going along just fine and then you're down and bleeding. But I was moving the other way with it. The great surprise to me was how tough and resilient people tend to be.

You club them, you punch them, you stick them, you shoot them, and they just hang around. It doesn't really seem to matter what they have to live for—wives and children, a favorite hound, a momma at the home place—people just keep on going out of pluck or habit or spite.

Who the hell knew? I found myself thinking it was all a little inspiring.

"He's going to be pissed," Luther assured me.

"Only gear he's got."

EIGHTEEN

Desmond rolled up early and tried to come in the apartment, but the stockyard bouquet kept him on the landing. He just opened the door long enough to tell us all that he was there.

"Where are we heading?" Desmond asked me once I'd slipped outside.

"Not sure. The Braves lost. I couldn't get Eugene to talk any sense."

I told Desmond all about Dale and how he'd be looking now twice as hard.

"Kind of a tough few days for him," Desmond said, and we stood there being sympathetic for very nearly a half minute.

According to Eugene, Guy the diabolical meth lord didn't have what he'd call a regular home. He had houses and trailers all over where Mexicans cooked drugs for him, along with a couple of hunting camps and some sort of warehouse up near Batesville, but Eugene was of a mind that he rented that out.

"What I'm saying," Eugene told me, "is Guy ain't so easy to find."

"That's pretty much what I'm hearing. If you had to find him, how would you do it?"

"Call him maybe until he called me back."

"So call him."

"Phone's in the bayou," Eugene told me. "It knew his number. I don't."

"All right. So what if you can't call him?"

"I'd look at his places and maybe ask his Mexicans."

"What do they know?"

"Maybe nothing, but sometimes they hear shit."

"First stop?"

"Probably his house out by Fitler. I drink Pepsis with the boys down there. Ain't but kids. Two wetbacks. White guy's a meth head."

"I've got an uncle on Baconia Road," Percy Dwayne piped in. "It's down around there, too. If Sissy'd decided she'd had enough of Guy, that's probably the first place she'd go. Can we swing by for a minute? It's right on the way."

I nodded, couldn't really see the harm.

We took off in the truck with Desmond and Luther

following us in the Geo. Eugene took some crazy route back through the countryside. He crossed a few main arteries, but he'd never ride on one. He had a real knack for finding the raggedest thoroughfares in the Delta. I spent half my time airborne since there weren't any seat belts about. Eugene had the steering wheel holding him down. The rest of us weren't so lucky.

"What have you got against asphalt?" I finally asked him.

Eugene just laughed and turned by a wheat field. I caromed off the roof of the cab.

"He ain't legal," Tommy said.

"You've got a tag," I told him. "I saw it."

"Yeah, well," Eugene said, "that ain't exactly mine."

"So you're hauling around what? Ephedrine and ether? On a stolen tag? Ever hear about those killers who get caught from parking tickets?"

"That'd be some shit, wouldn't it?" Eugene said, and then added, "I'm careful where I park."

Just then we met a state trooper in a turn not big enough for us both. We crowded him out, and he went off the road and mired up in a makeshift rice paddy—a ditch full of water with a foot and half of Delta mud underneath.

It didn't take a psychic to see what Eugene was thinking. It was along the lines of "I'm getting the fuck out of here."

As he stomped on the gas, I reached over and threw the shifter into neutral, which Eugene got all wide-eyed and incredulous about.

"We run," I told him in a low, hissed whisper, "and every one of his buddies'll be scouring the Delta for us. Can't just leave him here like nothing happened." I paused to come up with likeliest story I could. "We're going to pick up tractor tires. We're sorry as hell for what we did."

It was something to watch. Three Delta hoodlums trying to be contrite out of handcuffs. That's a thing you don't get to see just every day. I took the lead a little there at the first because that trooper was hot and didn't much care who he barked at. He was fairly low wattage, even by state trooper standards, so I just had to shuffle and scratch and let the ire all boil away. At least Eugene and Tommy and Percy Dwayne were all gifted at looking pathetic.

That trooper was a Magnum, T. E., his tag said, and he was chafed about how some people drive, he told us.

"I was fooling with the radio," Eugene allowed. "Lord I've learned my lesson now."

I could see Desmond's Metro well back down the road. He'd been following us at a considerable distance. Otherwise he and Luther would have been buried in Eugene's dust.

He'd stopped where he was and just sat there idling, waiting. I saw Luther get out of the car. I watched Desmond pull him back in. Not gently, but quick and hard. Doubtless Luther had seen some Tasing prospects in our bit of bother.

We just had K-Lo's shotgun, which I had permission to have, but it was laid out on the floorboard looking a little too ready to go, and I didn't want to find myself quizzed about it. The object here was to keep that trooper thinking about himself and not worrying about us and what we might be up to.

"I'm sure we can pull you out," I told him. "It wouldn't be right if we didn't."

The boys all mumbled like they wouldn't among them object to doing what's right.

"We been hauling tires," Tommy said without anybody asking.

"Tractor tires," Percy Dwayne added. "Running empty right now."

T. E. Magnum looked from one to the other. He seemed to think we were all simple, and before Eugene could tack on something impertinent himself, I said, "Go get your chain, Buddy. Got one in the bed, don't you?"

Eugene nodded and said, "Use it sometimes. You know. For tractor tires and such."

They were a sight with their suit coats and all. They didn't look like they had sense enough to get hired hauling any-thing. Fortunately, though, T. E. Magnum was a preening fool himself, and he was worried chiefly about getting Delta mud on his uniform trousers. So I told him to climb on into his cruiser and we'd take care of the rest.

I got stuck hooking the chain to the chassis because Pearl hadn't insisted on me any of Gil's clothes. I was wearing the sort of grungy togs a fellow could get muddy in. Nobody said as much, but I'd still be standing there with that chain in hand if I'd waited for somebody to offer to do what I ended up doing myself.

"Think you can drive?" I said to Eugene, and he climbed in under the wheel. "Don't go until I tell you."

"Right, Chief," he said, and laid hard on the gas.

T. E. Magnum didn't have to do a thing but try and avoid whiplash. Eugene jerked him out of that rice field as nice as you please. It might have been easier on his cruiser if he'd had the chance to shift out of park, but Eugene only dragged him about ten yards or so.

He finally stopped and backed up enough for me to unhook the chain, and I got between T. E. Magnum and the tag on Eugene's truck and went about apologizing as tediously as I could manage. When I got to the part about my daddy being laid up and sick, that trooper got bored, gave me a finger wave, and raced away toward Desmond. He would have put Desmond in the ditch if Desmond hadn't been sitting still.

"You're about the worst liars I've ever seen."

They weren't troubled or offended.

"Don't need to lie much," Tommy said.

Eugene ground the gears and got us going. "That's why we're way back here."

I'd been thinking about it wrong. Eugene and Tommy, even Percy Dwayne, were the sort who either went scot-free or got brought up on charges. Clean away or caught. There wasn't any middle course where you had to talk yourself out of

trouble. People knew what you did or they didn't. Somebody
had sworn out a warrant or not. It had a kind of integrity to
it and couldn't really get much simpler.

So I didn't say anything else to Eugene about taking the
local blacktops. I just braced myself against the cab roof and
tried to keep from levitating.

NINETEEN

Percy Dwayne's uncle on Baconia Road lived with a woman who wasn't Percy Dwayne's aunt. The house was hers. The dachshunds were hers. The clutter in the front yard was hers. The Nissan was hers. The toolshed was hers. The self-propelled Toro was hers. Every damn nickel they collected so they'd have two to rub together came due to a job she hated but showed up to every day.

To hear it from her, Percy Dwayne's uncle didn't do a blessed thing, which explained why he didn't point out to us everything that was his.

"Go on, tell them what's yours," the woman who wasn't Percy Dwayne's aunt insisted.

Percy Dwayne's uncle drew on his Pall Mall. He grinned and told us, "Nothing."

That wasn't strictly true, not anymore. Percy Dwayne had remedied that. Just the day before he'd brought his uncle and the woman who wasn't his aunt a forty-two-inch plasma television. They were watching it when the uncle opened the door and let us into what wasn't his house.

He wasn't actually married to the woman who wasn't Percy Dwayne's aunt but was just living with her strictly due to her merciful dispensation. In return she seemed to have seized the right to belittle and emasculate him in a casual and almost sporting sort of way.

Percy Dwayne called his uncle Doodle, but the woman who wasn't Percy Dwayne's aunt only ever referred to him as "this shitbag here." For his part, Doodle just grinned and smoked, while Percy Dwayne was left to defend his uncle's character.

In this case, the uncle was suitably older than Percy Dwayne, but the woman who wasn't Percy Dwayne's aunt kept telling us she was just thirty. As claims go, it seemed wishful based on the evidence at hand.

Her bare feet looked to be forty-five and her spider-veined legs about sixty. She had a lot more girth than her housedress had been built to handle, so she was leaking out of it where the seams were weak and everywhere else there was a hole. She had jowly underarms and fifteen or twenty necks, a meth addict's smile (a lot more gum than enamel), and a shade of hair on the order of a groundhog in July.

If one of the things she owned was a vacuum cleaner, she must not have held it dear, because Eugenia (her name was) and Uncle Shitbag were parked right in the middle of domestic squalor on a monumental scale.

Eugenia and Uncle Shitbag were living among Banquet chicken boxes, hamburger wrappers, burrito sleeves, and empty malt liquor forties. Their dog companions were so fat and aged that they could barely walk. Worse still, they weren't regular dachshunds. They were the long-haired miniature sort, which usually come with gastrointestinal defects and deplorable attitudes.

So while I was casting around for something redeeming about Percy Dwayne's uncle and the woman who wasn't his aunt, they were frustrating me at every turn with their prattle and shiftlessness. Eugenia mostly since Doodle made do as a whiskery affirmation. She'd announce some thought she was having about one thing or another, and he'd nod and say, "Lot of truth to that."

Most of it was Fox News–related. They had their forty-two-inch plasma set tuned to the Fox late-morning news. Effervescent talk about jihadists and the liberal seditionist front.

Eugenia informed us in no uncertain terms that her and Uncle Shitbag hadn't heard a peep out of Percy Dwayne's wife, and she went on to wonder about a man who couldn't control his woman.

"Don't you?" she asked Percy Dwayne's uncle, and in a sign of, I guess, affection she reached out and tugged on his ear like she was hoping to pull it off.

●

This time Uncle Doodle cackled and smoked and said back to Eugenia, "Angel's pissing."

One of the dachshunds was irrigating a Hardee's bag on the floor. Eugenia threw Uncle Shitbag's ashtray at it, which helped account for how the house had gotten the way it was.

Percy Dwayne's uncle rose from the couch and picked his way toward the kitchen. He gave us a sort of wink as if to invite us to follow him there. We did to the extent the three of us could fit inside the kitchen, where they were making compost and penicillin together and at once.

Doodle nodded and whispered, "She called this morning. That one"—he said of Eugenia—"was on the crapper."

"What did she say?" Percy Dwayne asked him.

"Couldn't say much, I don't guess. He was hanging around her. I could hear him. And that baby of yours was crying."

"Was she looking for me?"

"Didn't really get that far. She was looking to find somebody who wasn't him."

"Where is she?" I asked.

"I don't know," Doodle told me.

"You know anything about Guy?"

Doodle glanced toward the front room. He motioned for us to follow him out the back kitchen door and onto the porch. It appeared to have been a screen porch once but was now a sort of dumpster where all the rubbish that wouldn't fit in the house ended up.

"She had kind of a problem," Doodle told us, by which he meant Eugenia, and he went on to give us some details about the people she'd run with, the narcotics she'd favored, the trouble she'd found, the redemption she'd finally won. "She's a Christian woman now."

That surprised me a little. She'd not impressed me as Christian but more as a petty, sneering, and self-deluded witch.

"She's all cleaned up," Doodle told us. I had to think malt liquor didn't count. "She used to do some work for that son of a bitch."

"Guy?"

Doddle nodded. "She seen him do shit to people. Treat them like dogs."

"Did you know any of this?" I asked Percy Dwayne.

"I couldn't stop her," he told me, and shook his head. "Sissy's always liked her men bad."

"Mine too," Doodle said of Eugenia. "But she's off it anymore."

"Know where we can find him?" I asked Doodle.

"He's all over the damn place. I can tell you this, got a house over in Fitler near the river. One of the boys cooking that shit for him over there isn't a goddamn Mexican. Fellow from up by Nitta Yuma. Good as put his daddy in the ground."

"Who?" Percy Dwayne asked.

"That middle Hobart boy."

"The one with the birthmark?" Percy Dwayne asked as he pressed his palm to his cheek.

Doddle nodded. "That shit got hold of him. You won't even know who you're looking at."

"The one that played the fiddle?"

"Yeah, well," Doodle told him. "He don't play it no more."

"We were already on our way there," I said.

"What are you packing?" Doodle wanted to know.

Short of a shoulder-fired rocket, I don't think I could have satisfied him.

"I'll fix you up," he said.

He went in a closet and brought out a gun wrapped in a towel. It was an authentic M4A1, the Colt model for Special Forces and an awful hell of a long way from Fort Bragg.

"Where did you get this?" I asked him.

"Got a buddy."

"Is he the Secretary of Defense?"

I hadn't held one in a few years, but got comfortable with it quick. I ejected the clip and checked the movement. Uncle Doodle's had the pistol grip.

"Damn," Percy Dwayne said.

"Damn's right," I told him. "You could cut Guy and all of his buddies right in half with this."

There was a sweetgum tree in the backyard. It was framed by the porch doorway where there wasn't anything but an unscreened panel anymore. I let go a burst into the trunk. The dachshunds started howling, followed close on by Eugenia. Desmond came around the house at full glide with his machine pistol in hand.

Uncle Doodle looked from me with his M4 to Desmond with his Steyr. "I think you boys'll be all right," he said.

Doodle supplied us with two full clips. I paused in the

front room to take the blame for the gunfire and temporarily get Uncle Shitbag off the hook.

"That's an awful nice TV," I told Eugenia, and it looked a lot better sitting in Eugenia's TV cabinet than it had on the floor of Percy Dwayne and Sissy's house two days before.

"He gave it to us," she said, and glared at Percy Dwayne. "I don't know why." She made it sound like an accusation.

Percy Dwayne was standing right beside me, not breathing at all. I'm sure he thought I was going to repo the thing. A day or two earlier, I might have, but I had other things than televisions on my mind just then.

"That's a thoughtful gift," I told Eugenia. "You and Doodle here enjoy it."

Eugenia snorted and said, "Can't imagine why I'd be needing you to tell me what to do."

"That's right. Hobart," Eugene said when we repeated what Doodle had told us. "They call him Slim. He's about as ruined as they come."

"Maybe we can help him."

"Yeah," Eugene told me as he pointed at the M4. "Take that thing and shoot him in the head."

"Sure you know what you're doing?" Tommy asked me.

"Guy's got you boys rattled," I said.

"He ain't like any of you," Eugene told us. "He'll do any damn thing to any damn body as easy as you breathe."

"Evil bastard?"

Eugene and Tommy nodded vigorously.

I couldn't help but think how much I preferred evil to shiftlessness. Evil has form and purpose. Evil has logic, even if it's warped. Evil is unconflicted. It's dependable and thorough. You never run across people who are only evil half the time.

Shiftlessness doesn't have anything but a galling lack of pluck. It's mindless and almost incidental. You can't be shiftless and evil, just like you can't be shiftless and decent. Think of the commitment, the troublesome responsibility. When you go up against evil people, they drive all your doubt away.

They followed us in the Geo, Luther and Desmond did, and I let Percy Dwayne get behind the wheel of the truck. Eugene was suffering through a moderate collapse of nerve, and he was contaminating Tommy with his runaway misgivings. It was like we were going to pay a call on Lucifer at home.

We took back roads down to Blanton and then the regular highway to Onward where Percy Dwayne turned west toward Fitler and the river on Route 1. By then, Eugene had worked himself into a certifiable state. He wondered who'd take care of his dogs and keep up his house when he was dead. Would they even find his body so they could put him in a grave?

"What did you see?" I finally asked him.

"Nothing," he lied.

"Look at yourself. You're giving us everything but the story."

"I saw a man killed," Eugene finally said.

And Percy Dwayne told him sneeringly, "Shit."

Percy Dwayne added how he'd seen all sorts of people done away with. Drunk behind the wheel. Shot. Stabbed. Beat with bats and such.

"Where?" I asked Percy Dwayne.

"All over," he told me. "The Delta's a funny place."

"This was different," Eugene said.

"D-d-different," Tommy added and nodded.

"Did you see it, too?" I asked him.

"Naw, but I heard about it once."

"Can't sit on it now," I told Eugene.

He said he didn't guess he could. "Shouldn't even have been there. Having truck trouble. Couldn't get no spark."

"Where exactly?"

"One of Guy's places. Down near Eagle Bend. Back on Steele Bayou in the scrub. He was having a problem with one of his slingers—some boy from over in Jackson. Skimming or something. I don't know. It don't take much with Guy."

Then Eugene got busy directing Percy Dwayne off a perfectly good paved road. He sent him down a track in the middle of a soybean field toward a row of trees that looked ten miles away.

"Guy killed him?" I asked.

"After a while. Just started in cutting him up."

The road was washed out from the field irrigation, and Percy Dwayne failed to slow down until we'd all been just about flung clear of the truck.

"Creep a little," I told him.

Even he'd bounced off the cab roof by then and so thought I might be talking sense.

"Guy's got this knife," Eugene said. He held his hands a foot and a half apart. "Some Japanese thing he took off a fellow. He strops it to keep it sharp. It's always around him somewhere, and he pulled it out of his car when him and that boy were having words. He just lopped that fellow's arm off right there at the elbow, and suddenly Guy didn't seem mad anymore."

"Shit!" Percy Dwatne said. "Whacked a boy's arm clean off?"

Eugene nodded. "Yes sir," he said. "Right through gristle and bone, every damn thing. Like he was taking apart a fryer."

Tommy nodded. Tommy said, "Yes sir," too.

"Funny thing about Guy," Eugene went on. "He can get as pissed off as anybody, but you and me would get stirred up and do harm *because* we were mad. Then we'd be sorry about it. That's the way with people, isn't it? People I know anyway. You chop a fellow's arm off, the next thing you're going to do is wish you hadn't."

"I hear you," Percy Dwayne said. "You ain't telling me a thing."

"This wasn't that," Eugene insisted. "Two boys can get to fighting, and it can go bad. But this was something else. This was Guy's sort of fun."

Eugene said he was pulling spark plugs when that boy let out a shriek. He looked over just as Guy bent down and plucked that boy's arm off the ground. They were standing just off the bayou, not ten yards from the water, and Eugene said Guy took that length of arm and tossed it right on in.

"His gator must have been there waiting. He had one he fed goats to, and the water started churning and boiling. Guy whipped around with knife of his and set to whacking at that boy again. He took off his other arm up near the shoulder."

It was the laughing that got to Eugene. Guy was having a grand time, and the more that boy screamed and bled, the happier Guy seemed to get.

"I'd known Guy a little while by then. We'd played some poker together. He'd laugh at the table when you'd tell him a joke, and this was just like that. Fun," Eugene told us. "Just something to do."

"Jesus," Percy Dwayne said, and it was easy enough to tell he was thinking of his wife and son. "Yesterday he seemed like anybody. But smooth, you know. A little slicker than regular people."

"That's the thing about Guy," Eugene told us all. "He fits in until he don't."

Eugene couldn't get his truck to turn over. "I half figured I was next. He was having a high time taking that boy to pieces and feeding him bit by bit to that stinking alligator. It looked like the fellow was a third in the swamp before he finally died. Guy all covered in blood and laughing like the devil's own first cousin. And those boys of his, you know . . ." Eugene turned to Tommy.

"Big guys," Tommy said. "Muscles all over."

"They didn't look like they were caring for it, either. But they didn't try to stop Guy. No sir. Didn't say a thing."

Eugene said the worst of it was when Guy came over to him.

"Blood everywhere, all over him, but he didn't seem to care. He's got that knife in his hand, big shiny thing, I'm standing there on the bumper wondering if I'd even feel it when it passed through my neck."

Eugene shook his head and gave a little quiver like he was having a chill. "'What's your trouble?' Guy asked me." Eugene laughed. "What's my fucking trouble, and him standing there looking like he'd been dipped in guts. What's my trouble? Shit."

"What did you tell him?" Percy Dwayne wanted to know.

"Told him it didn't have no spark. He reached in and wiggled a wire or two. He don't know shit about cars. Said Gary would take me home and I could come back for the truck. I figured Gary would haul me a couple of miles, put me out, and shoot me dead."

"Must not have," Percy Dwayne said.

"No. Dropped me off about a half mile from the house, afraid he'd get mired up. Didn't say a word to me on the way. Gary never was a talker. I was getting out when he finally asked me if I'd ever wondered what hell was like."

"What did you tell him?"

Eugene shrugged. "Said I'd heard it was hot or something. After that night, I never saw Gary again."

"He quit?" I asked him.

"You don't quit Guy. He probably got a whiff of what was going on in Gary's head. He's pretty good about that sort of thing, can tell what everybody's thinking. And it was just Gary. There's lots more where he came from. He's probably passed through that gator by now."

I was coming to think I'd have to treat Guy about like I'd treat a rattler—stay out of his reach if I could manage it and brain him if I couldn't. He wasn't impressing me as the sort you could hope to reason with. I knew we were heading for the brand of trouble that just might get ugly fast.

Eugene directed Percy Dwayne onto a side road into a grove. Pecans and oaks and cottonwoods down where a church used to be. There was a bit of stone foundation left and a couple of wooden grave markers. Desmond pulled in behind us, and we all piled out and stretched.

Eugene pointed through the trees. I could just make out the glint off a propane tank.

"House is up through there. I'd leave it be," he said. "You haven't done a thing yet you can't undo."

TWENTY

"I trust you," I said to Eugene and Tommy, "but only up to a point."

Desmond pulled the coil wire off the truck and the one off the Geo as well, and I told Eugene and Tommy they could stick where they were or walk out if they had to.

"I don't give a shit," Eugene said, "as long as I'm not going over there."

Over there was through a wheat field and beyond it a scrubby hedgerow. Past that was just a house like a lot of houses out in the Delta—single floor frame on fieldstone pilings in the middle of nowhere much.

I gave Percy Dwayne the shotgun, kept the M4 for myself. Desmond had the Steyr on a sling over his shoulder.

Luther had left his double-breasted suit coat in the Metro and had his school bus–yellow Taser in hand. We weren't the magnificent seven exactly. More like the middling four, and it didn't help that we had to hold up at the near edge of the wheat field while I argued Desmond out of walking around it instead of through.

"You don't know what's in there," Desmond told me.

"Wheat," I said.

But Desmond had reptiles on his mind and was lobbying for a detour, which looked to me about a mile away.

"I'll go first," I told him. "You walk behind me."

"What if you get bit?"

"I'm guessing you'll turn around."

Of course, now I had reptiles on my mind, but I suppose that was better than worrying about getting fed to an alligator, especially in bite-sized pieces carved off by a maniac.

After about thirty yards, the setting took over, and I lost my interest in snakes. We were thigh-deep in luxurious wheat in a field that covered three or four hundred acres. It flat disappeared off to the north and ran to a far hedgerow on the south end. The sky overhead was bright spring blue instead of the scorching white it went to in the full heat of summer. The wheat had that limey color that hardly looks natural and real.

It was a spectacular place to be. Life on the ground doesn't get much more vivid, but then I'd shift the M4 from one hand to the other and remember what we were about.

Maybe halfway across the field we started hearing the music. It was hardly the sort of stuff you'd expect to find pouring out of a meth house. Not rap or metal or techno funk rubbish but Scottish fiddle music. Airs and jigs on viola and guitar.

I was tempted at first to believe it was that ruined Hobart playing. That was a foolish fantasy, of course. I'd seen enough of meth in Virginia to know the furious power it had in a life for crowding out everything else. Of course that Hobart had long since sold his fiddle. It was a wonder he still had a boom box.

We slipped out of the wheat at a hedgerow on the far side of the field. It was a stand of trees three or four deep, mostly slender ash and elm, with a view across the junky back lot of a shabby bungalow. The building had that low, squat look of a former Delta commissary, a store where farmhands for many decades had bartered off their wages for overpriced foodstuffs and supplies.

They're a common sight in the Delta, low and sturdy, used now for storage mostly and the occasional residence. They're thought quaint these days and historical like the slave cabins people rent for weekends, all sun-bleached and spartan on the outside but pure rococo within.

You haven't really lived until you've seen a pasty Hattiesburg attorney sitting out on the porch of a refitted slave shack in his Bermuda shorts and loafers, running with sweat from the stark exertion of draining a Michelob.

The place in front of us, at least, was operating in the spirit of profiteering, which was the reason the thing had been built in the first place. It struck me as appropriate that it would end essentially like it had started.

We could hear people every now and again. Not talking so much but mostly shifting and rustling like mice in a wall. The occasional tinny clatter of pots banging. The sound of the front screen slamming as they went in and out of the building to get away from the fumes. And then the music, of course, lovely and with a highland melancholy. Not as out of place as you might think.

"So?" Desmond said.

"I can't imagine they're armed," I told him. "What would be the point? Fire a gun in that place, the whole house'll go up. I can smell the ether from here."

We had fertilizer funk and caustic pesticide stink off the field behind us, but it was no match for what was coming out of that house. Ether and ammonia and lye and acid. Methamphetamine might be slow poison finished and refined, but uncooked and in its component parts, it's the makings of a terrorist plot.

"You can't use that," I told Luther, pointing at his Taser. "No guns. No spark. No nothing. Got it?"

Luther nodded and then he went all drug-dealer indignant, went chattering on about how a man was obliged to draw a line. He seemed to believe he was on the side of the drug-slinging angels and that Acadian fuck stick was well off the other way.

I have to say, the distinction between meth and OxyContin

wasn't so clear to me as it appeared to be to Luther. But then all of us can convince ourselves of almost anything.

"Think they got money in there?" Percy Dwayne wanted to know.

"Nope," Desmond told him.

"Got to work our way to the money," I said. "This is just where it starts."

We went sneaking up to the back of the house with the propane tank for cover. I peeked in a window on a room that was vacant except for scattered muriatic acid jugs and a few empty Mason jar boxes. I'd decided that me and Desmond would be the only ones in the house. Luther was just too Taser-happy, and I half feared Percy Dwayne would go all vengeful husband on those boys.

So Desmond and I broke off to the left and circled around front that way while Luther and Percy Dwayne, hanging close to the sidewall, approached the front porch from the right. Me and Desmond climbed the rickety stairs to the decking and waited on either side of the front door until we'd heard enough to piece together what was going on inside.

There were three of them, like we'd figured. Two speaking Spanish, but only briefly and occasionally, the other one only coughing every now again. Fits of phlegmy hacking, which he'd punctuate and annotate with a "Whew!" or a "Well, shit!"

I was reaching for the screen door pull when we heard footsteps approaching, so I drew back and waited. A bare arm pushed open the door and a fellow came out. He looked maybe twenty, was hardly over five feet tall. He didn't appear so much Mexican as Mayan. Kind of café au lait, thick but not stout, and surprised to see us but in a passive and unflustered sort of way.

He was wearing shorts and shower shoes along with a paper face mask, the kind they sell in the hardware store that protects you from nothing much.

I jerked him clear of the doorway and pressed him against the siding, covered his face mask with my hand in case he was tempted to call out or yell.

He just looked at me like he couldn't imagine what I was doing there.

I suspect he'd long since made a perfectly rational calculation. He was out in the middle of nowhere cooking meth for a psychotic, so the chances of anybody showing up other than to butcher him for sport (given the tireless homicidal way that psychotics are known to work) were probably about as slim as they could get.

So once he'd glanced at me and Desmond and satisfied himself that we weren't Guy, he seemed prepared to be okay with whatever we were up to.

"English?" I asked him, leaning close and whispering in his ear.

"*Sí.*"

"How many inside?"

He held up two fingers.

"Call one out, in español."

He did a winning job of it, chattered out an invitation to

his buddy who threw open the screen and failed to yelp when I grabbed him and drew him over. I didn't even need to press a hand on his mask. I waved Luther over to where they could see him and directed those two boys down the stairs.

They both pulled their masks up onto their heads and stood in the yard in their shorts and flip-flops. They seemed interested in finding out what we'd be up to next. Not fretful about it but curious and pleased to have a break in their day.

I reasoned it'd be best to go inside and grab the last one, so I eased in with Desmond gliding up behind me.

The décor was a lot like at Percy Dwayne's house except for the staggering stink. The smell was little short of overpowering, and I revised my assessment of that pair of Mexicans. They weren't calm so much as addled. I'd been inside thirty seconds when my eyes started stinging and tearing so that I could hardly see.

We picked our way through the front room trash and fairly blundered into the kitchen. I think all either one of us wanted by then was to get the hell out of the house.

That Hobart was wearing just underwear. He was standing at the range against the far wall. His bare back was to us, and it and his legs were covered with sores. Some fresh and raw. Others scabbed over. More than a few were dark scars. His bony shoulder blades looked like they might just break through his skin.

He couldn't hear us for the music, didn't have any sense that we were there. He just stood at the stove swaying a little, maybe to the jig that was coming from the boom box. Maybe on account of the fumes.

"Hey, buddy," I said.

Not a dent on his end. He just swayed and stayed where he was.

"Hey!" I said, with volume this time, and he finally turned and saw us. Front on he was a ghastly sight. He looked like an actively rotting cadaver. All ribs and ruptured flesh. There was a wine stain covering his left cheek, and he didn't appear to have any teeth left. The meth had eaten away at his chin line as well so that he looked like Jacob Marley's ghost.

He glanced from me to Desmond and back again.

"Hey," he told us both.

We each took an arm and hauled him out, though Desmond and I together were both a little reluctant to touch his skin.

Once we had them all in the front yard in the shade of a pecan tree, I went back inside with Luther, and we picked a little through the litter, not that we expected to find any sign of Guy. There was a typewritten meth recipe, with amounts and specific procedures, taped to the inside of one of the kitchen cabinet doors. Otherwise it was all just wrappers and trash and tickets from the propane guy.

I grabbed the boom box and a couple of CD cases off the counter. It turned out that Hobart had been listening to Bonnie Rideout. Airs and jigs and *piobaireachds* to accompany the meth.

"Now what?" Luther asked me.

I glanced around, found an unopened bottle of ether. It was proper hospital stock, not spray starter from the auto supply. If there's such a thing as high-grade meth, Guy's boys were making it.

I showed that bottle to Luther. I told Luther, "Boom."

Percy Dwayne was out in the front yard quizzing those boys a little, but they weren't equipped to tell him anything.

The Mexicans were all shrugs and a chorus of *no se*s while that Hobart slouched and gazed around like he didn't know where he was.

"Got a car?" I asked.

The first boy out, the one with the English, said, "Uh-uh."

"How do you come and go?"

He told me they walked to the road and his mother picked them up.

"Whose mother?" I asked him

He pointed at that Hobart.

"She knows he's here?"

He nodded like I was slower than he'd hope for.

And there I'd been thinking how sweet it would be to carry that Hobart home to his mother. She'd nurse him and help to break his habit. She'd bring him back to fiddle shape. What a rich and rewarding and, come to find out, purely fictional thing that would be.

"How does a mother even stand to look at that?"

"Mother, hell," Luther told me, "I can't hardly take it myself."

"What are we going to do with them?" Desmond asked me.

"Carry them up the road, I guess." I turned to the Mexicans and asked, "Where's home?"

The one with the English misunderstood me. I meant where in the Delta. He drew himself up to his full five feet, smiled, and told me, "Tegucigalpa."

"Where the fuck's that?" Percy Dwayne asked.

"Them Mexicans," Desmond told him, "ain't Mexicans after all."

Everybody went but me. Through the hedgerow and into the wheat. I dumped out that bottle of ether on the naked front room planking. I stood at the front door and fired a burst from that M4. The spark ignited the fumes and the ether caught with a *POOFT*. I didn't wait around for what was coming next but lit out for the wheat myself.

I was maybe twenty yards into the field when the house simply exploded. The roof lifted and walls blew out. A jet of flame shot into the air. The heat hit me almost immediately, came in a gust that moved the wheat.

Drawn by the spectacle, three crop dusters converged in the vicinity. Two canary Ag Cats and a red Air Tractor circled the destruction like flies over cow flop. It was just the sort of thing Guy would hear about straightaway and maybe write off as the cost of doing business. Until, that is, they failed to turn up incinerated employees.

It took a hell of a lot longer to get back across that wheat field than it had going out. That ratty, meth-eaten Hobart kept wandering off or stopping altogether. He didn't seem to know what he was up to from one minute to the next. The sun appeared to dazzle and distract him, and he kept running his hands through the wheat as if he couldn't quite figure what it might be and how he'd come to be in it.

I like a good obliterating bender about as much as the next guy, but once you've hung it on hard and forgotten for maybe a night just who you are, there's something reassuring about waking up dinged and sober. I couldn't be wasted all the time. It would be staggering misery.

That Hobart, though, didn't function that way. He was the happiest meth head I've ever seen. He was one of those guys who can only tolerate this world when he's high. You could see it in his face. Standing in the middle of that wheat field, bathed in late May sunlight and surrounded by limey green as far as you could see, he was so delighted he could barely bring himself to move. His smile was gummy, like a toddler's, but it was sure as shit a smile.

Everybody else went on ahead while I stayed behind to squire that Hobart. The whole enterprise had gotten surreal by then. The house well behind us was crackling and popping. The planes were all still circling. That Hobart was soaking in the world like he'd never been outside before.

I wanted him to hurry along a little, but I didn't want to touch him. He was bony and blistered and seeping here and there. It was bad enough walking beside him without having to lay on hands.

So I just drove him like I'd drive a cow. I slung the M4 by its strap. I held out my free arm, the one without the boom box, and clicked my tongue to encourage him along. It succeeded after a while. There near the end, he saw Eugene over in the church lot standing next to his truck. The sight was something familiar to him and had the effect of pulling him on.

Once we'd finally cleared the field, that Hobart shuffled over to Eugene and told him "Hey" with what looked like some variety of affection.

"Hey here, buddy," Eugene said back.

"What are we doing?" that Hobart asked him.

Eugene glared my way. "Fuck if I can say."

"You only ever work *here?*" I asked the Mexican with English who was actually Honduran.

He'd become local to the extent that he said, "Naw." Then he told me about another two houses of Guy's that he worked in, too.

"Where?" I asked him.

He pointed at Eugene. "He knows," he said.

Eugene had been letting on that he was fuzzy up until then. Didn't have any details, couldn't recall where anything was. Been to a place or two once or twice, didn't imagine he could locate them again. Come to find out from my Mexican friend from Tegucigalpa that Eugene knew an awful lot more than he'd let on.

"So you do know," I said to Eugene. "You know it all."

"I just drive and deliver shit," he told me. "Why the hell did you get me into this?"

"Because I had a 1969 calypso coral Ranchero. You helped it go away, and you're going to help bring it back."

"It's just a goddamn car!"

"That's not for you to say. Load these boys up and let's take them out of here."

We found we couldn't trust that Hobart to ride in the back of Eugene's truck. He kept wanting to wander out of the bed, so we brought him into the cab and put Tommy back with the Mexican/Hondurans, which Tommy complained bitterly about.

Those boys from Tegucigalpa took Tommy as he was and seemed happy to be out in the midday air, even if it was with a swamp rat.

We ended up carrying the three of them to that Hobart's mother's house. It was a tidy little thing up near Nitta Yuma in a grove of pecan trees. She had a glider in the yard and a flower bed. Painted rocks along the driveway. Cucumbers growing in pots. That Hobart's mother came out at the sound of Eugene's jackleg truck pulling up the drive.

I don't know what I expected. Filthy housecoat. Glass of bourbon. Horns. She was something else entirely, a sort of oblivious throwback. We might have just rolled into 1945. She had on a cotton apron with daisies all over it, and underneath was the kind of shift that housekeepers used to wear. Gray with piping and a starched white collar. She was wearing hose and shoes so sensible they were crowding orthopedic.

"Well, Lord," she said, still smiling even after big black

Desmond had climbed out of his coupe. "Danny, why didn't you tell me you were bringing friends?"

The first thought that popped into my head was that she was smoking something, too. It turned out she was just blinkered by nature. She'd probably started practical and a little more tuned in but had turned away from all of that to cope.

I was the one who ended up having the fantasy exchange with her since everybody else was a little too thunderstruck by her behavior to talk. We helped her son out of the truck, and she planted a big kiss on his scabby cheek. She didn't appear to notice the sores, the ravaged physique, the dingy underwear.

"I'm making cobbler!" she told him about as brightly as Betty Crocker herself.

The Mexican/Hondurans climbed out of the bed, and she clapped her hands and greeted them as well. She seemed to know them as Hank and Grady. She told them about the cobbler, too.

I told her the boys were getting a half day off on account of Jefferson Davis's birthday.

"Isn't that nice," she said. "They all work so hard."

I'd rolled up despising the woman and planning to uncork a scalding thing or two, but seeing her standing there in her tidy yard in front of her tidy house with her doomed son and his immigrant coworkers, I discovered I could sympathize with what she was about.

It turned out her husband had dropped dead a couple of

years back. He'd had a coronary in the parking lot at the bank. Borrowing money to put their boy in rehab one more time.

She told me all about it, lingered on the part where she was making shortcake when the phone call came in.

"Daddy loved his shortcake, didn't he, honey?" she called to her son, who'd wandered out in the pecan grove at the bottom of the lot by then. He didn't appear to have an opinion about his father and shortcake.

We got invited to stay for cobbler and tea, but allowed as how we couldn't manage it at the moment, and we left that Hobart and his Honduran colleagues in the hands of that Hobart's mother who was worrying over her irises—velvety and midnight black—as we returned to the truck and the Geo down at the bottom of the drive.

I watched as the boys from Tegucigalpa strolled down among the pecans to fetch back that Hobart who'd wandered close to the road. That Hobart's mother called out after them, all bubbly and light. Her high-pitched laugh from this distance sounded a little like breaking glass.

"That boy'll be dead in a month or two," Luther said. "You think she even knows?"

"I'm guessing if she knows anything," I told him, "she knows that."

TWENTY-ONE

I laid it all out for Eugene—Tommy, too, since he was right there. "You sort of get to pick sides," I told them both, "except I'm going to help you."

Eugene went on at some length about how he didn't want any trouble, just hauled chemicals and shit, picked up what he was told, and took it where he was ordered, made a habit of not looking at what he didn't guess he should see. It was one of those traditional cracker explanations you hear whenever you catch one in an incriminating spot.

"I know you think you see me," is what Eugene was saying, "but the truth of the thing is I'm not really here."

"No more Guy after today. We're taking him out of the picture one way or another."

"Heard that before," Eugene informed me and added beyond it, "Shit."

Eugene and Tommy were mired together in a philosophical quandary. They were trying to piece together how best to save their wretched asses without doing anything they couldn't—if things went sideways—recover from.

They came up with a game they wanted me to play. I'd name little crappy desolate wide spots in the Delta, and Eugene would tell me whether or not there was one of Guy's houses there.

"I've got a better idea," I told him, and I took the barrel of Doodle's M4 and laid it against Eugene's left ear canal.

Eugene proved awfully good at my version of the game and had soon sent us on the way to a place called (honestly) Africa, Mississippi. Not Africa proper, but the outskirts of Africa on a branch of the Sunflower River, which seemed to run every damn where water could go.

This particular house was just a shack. It looked abandoned. Apparently Guy didn't let his cookers drive to work and park their cars. I wouldn't have guessed the place had power if I'd not seen the satellite dish. These boys weren't the boom box sort. They had an actual TV.

I took just Desmond and Percy Dwayne, left Tommy and Eugene with Luther and his school-bus yellow Taser. We came down along the riverbank and slipped up through what once had been a garden. That house was all unpainted cypress with half the front porch caved in. You had to climb a stepladder just to get in the door.

Those boys were watching an installment of *Law & Order*, Jerry Orbach vintage, and Jerry was right in the middle of a bon mot when I stepped in the front room proper and tried to ease across the floor. The whole structure squeaked and moaned so I was in fear it might collapse.

Desmond was at the top of the ladder, but I waved him off from coming in. I stepped into the kitchen just as those cookers were turning around to see who exactly was making the whole damn building jiggle and shake.

I didn't even have to raise my gun. I'd figured as much after the first place when nobody lifted a finger to do shit. The crew here was one Mexican and two black kids. They all looked eighteen or twenty, and they reacted identically to the fact I'd come to show them out.

"Fuck it," one of the black kids told me.

That was the prevailing view, and I advised them to take the television. The last we saw of those fellows they were walking down what looked like a deer track into a thicket, and the Mexican and one of the black kids were carrying a Samsung forty-two-incher between them.

This place had a little less ether inside but was hardly more than standing kindling, so we didn't attract any crop dusters, but the house burned and fell in quick. We beat it back to the vehicles, and then Eugene sent us over to Colby, which was east of the national forest, and this place was set back in a swamp.

It was a hell of a thing to get to. There was a trail down a hummocky stretch and then sagging planks over murky runs of water. I took Percy Dwayne and left Desmond halfway back once we'd found him a stump to stand on to get him up out of the scrub and away from the reptiles.

This house on the bayou was a lot like Eugene's, except a little less charming and sound. It's hard to get away with jack-leg construction in the middle of a swamp because there's nothing about to help anything planned and hand-built remain standing. Everything in a bayou works toward rot and destruction, and whoever had built this shack was either worthless or resigned and had ended up just helping nature along.

The place had a platform, but it was listing off to starboard. Somebody had tried to jack it up and firm it with cross braces, but the nails had pulled and the planks had warped and gravity had set back in. There didn't seem to be a power supply beyond a generator, a little portable one on skids that we'd been hearing all the while.

It was running rough, sputtering and coughing. It sounded like water in the gas, so the swamp was even spoiling that as well. It gave a last chug and quit as we were closing on the place.

We crossed a final board bridge and slipped up tight, eased in next to a piling. Just like the others, this one was a three-man operation. We could hear two voices from inside the shack, and the third man was out on the platform. He was fishing for turtles with what looked like a sizable hunk of nutria or rat.

He had a line, and a hook, and a seepy chunk of vermin

with a little pelt and an entire foot attached, and he was dangling it over a half-sunk log beneath him in the bayou.

We could see him through a gap in the decking. He looked a little like that Hobart, though not quite as far along. He was sinking into ruin and spoilage but could probably have passed for just ailing. His skin was sloughing off him, which was playing havoc with his tattoos, and he wasn't so scarred and ulcerated as that Hobart had been.

We were going to climb up and join him, but there weren't any stairs we could find. Percy Dwayne spied the extension ladder they'd hauled up behind them, so we had to go about it another way.

I got right under that boy on the deck. He was jiggling that line so that the rat's dead foot was bouncing, and he was singing softly. It was a jumpy tune I couldn't place at first, but it turned out to be the meth-head swamp-cracker version of "All the Single Ladies." I would as soon have expected selections from *Tosca* or a Weavers medley.

It was all so strange and wondrous, I almost hated to intervene.

"Hey," I said, and that boy looked around like he thought he'd heard somebody speak. Then he went back to jiggling his line and singing under his breath.

"Hey," I said. Now he was mystified and a little uneasy. He glanced around like maybe I was calling from the treetops.

"Down here," I told him, and he glanced at the decking and saw us through the crack.

"Call your buddies," I said. "Get them outside."

He grinned at me and spat my way. "Go on with you. We done pulled the ladder up."

I raised the M4 and fired a short burst straight up through the decking. It was crap wood to start with and saturated from the swamp, so the planks did more showy disintegrating than I'd anticipated. Beyoncé up top was suitably impressed.

The other two came out to see what all of the racket was about.

They were swamp rats as well. I guess the brothers and the Mexicans weren't so keen to work back in the bayou, so it was just five of us white boys eyeing each other through a hole in the platform.

"What the hell you doing?" one of the fellows from inside asked us.

"Put the goddamn ladder down," Percy Dwayne told him, and he decided for big-swinging-dick effect to let off a shotgun round.

Lucky for us, the underside of the decking was so soft that most of those rubber pellets just embedded and stuck. But a few of them went bouncing and zipping around, both under the deck and above it, which made us about as excited as we could stand at the moment.

"Damn, man," Beyoncé said. "Them things sting."

Percy Dwayne was more than ready to lord it over his brethren, so he raised K-Lo's shotgun and would have fired again if I'd not stopped him. I shoved my finger behind his trigger and called up, "Ladder. Now."

They dropped it down for us, and we climbed up, but that platform hadn't been engineered for six legitimate adults. It sagged and swayed so much that I sent Percy Dwayne and those boys down. That shack was like a treehouse kids would build with scraps. They'd been working off a hot plate inside and packaging the stuff out on the back edge of the deck. They'd set up a board for a table, had a kitchen scale and a Tuffy tub full of Baggies. It was all crystal and felt like maybe two or three pounds altogether. Enough to keep the local tweakers happy for a while.

"He ain't going to like this." That was Beyoncé talking.

"Probably not," I said, and I spilled some gas out of the generator and lit the deck on fire.

This place didn't explode like the first one or burn hot and quick like the second. It smoldered from all the damp and raised a cloud of blue-black smoke. I climbed down, and one of the inside boys said, "You going to kill us now?"

"How'd you get in here?"

He pointed at a flatboat over on the weedy bank.

"Go on," I told him. "I don't need you dead."

They took their sweet time getting the thing in the water. It had a little trolling motor on the back, and they fumbled a fair bit before they got the battery hooked up.

That gave them time for one of them to tell me, "He'll cut your fucking heart out." Not as a threat so much as a scrap of prognostication.

They got out maybe thirty yards before they fired upon us

with a rifle they'd had squirreled away in the boat. The bullet hit one of the pilings, and the whole structure quivered and shook.

"Why don't you give them one," I told Percy Dwayne. That was all he needed to hear.

Those rubber pellets came swarming at them out the barrel of K-Lo's Beretta, and those boys couldn't find the water fast enough.

Too bad for them they'd left their trolling motor running, and as me and Percy Dwayne crossed the plank bridge to get out, we could hear them blaming each for the boat taking off and beating about in the swamp.

Desmond had left his stump and returned to the car. He was leaning on the front fender and complained to me of being famished and weak. He'd been in consultation with Eugene, and they thought we were maybe thirty minutes from the Yazoo Sonic. That'd be like crossing the street anywhere else.

Desmond told me all this in a dry and tactical sort of way. It was coming on mid afternoon by then, and my plan, which had been loose and vindictive, was finally solidifying. I knew, though, I'd need Desmond at full strength to help me see it through.

"All right," I told him. "But get takeout. And I don't have any money."

"I want a corn dog," Percy Dwayne said to Desmond, "that nobody throws on the ground."

"You'll come find us," I said to Desmond, and then turned to Eugene. "Tell him where we're going to be."

"You've burned three of them already," Eugene said. "Don't you think that's enough? Must have got back to Guy by now."

"I want the best one. There must be one that's better than the others. One he's a little sentimental about."

"First one, maybe. Been running the longest. Up around Louise."

Then Desmond and Eugene had one of those take-the-branch-road-and-turn-at-the-grain-bin conversations before Desmond set off toward Yazoo, and Luther and Tommy drew lots to see who'd ride in the bed of the truck.

Luther won the cab, and on the way to Louise, he had more than a few things he wanted to wonder aloud about. Now that we were all in the shit with this crazy bastard Guy, Luther was hoping he could get me to lay out the future for him. Nothing long term, maybe just the balance of the afternoon.

"You've got a plan, right?"

I nodded. Truth be told, it was more of a trajectory than a plan.

"You're trying to bait him out?"

That was good, too, so I nodded at Luther again.

"Don't forget Sissy and PD," Luther said. "Got to figure out where they're at."

I nodded again. "Sissy and PD," I said.

"And what about the money?" Luther asked me. "He's bound to have piles of it somewhere."

"Yeah," I said and asked Eugene, "Where does the cash end up?"

"See, now you're getting into shit I just ain't supposed to know."

"Not supposed to know or don't know?" I asked him.

And Eugene made the kind of face that either meant he knew where the money was or he'd eaten a spoonful of earwax. "Tell me one thing for sure," Eugene said.

"Okay."

"You're going to kill him, right?"

"Could well come to that."

"Has to," Eugene told me. "That fellow just has to get dead."

"All right," I said.

Eugene looked left and and right like he was fearful of being overheard.

"Got a room where they count it and pack it up," he said.

"Where?"

"Guy's got a place over by the river, up around Blue Hole. That's where all the money ends up. Somebody's there all the time."

"Does he live there?"

"Sometimes. As often as any. It's kind of a hunting lodge back in the swamp."

"So once he gets nervous, that's where he'll end up?"

"I suppose," Eugene told me, "but he's not the nervous sort."

"Let's see what we can do about that," I said.

TWENTY-TWO

We were nearly to Louise when Eugene directed Percy
Dwayne back onto Rainbow Road and then off it down a
track by a catfish farm. A dozen rectangular ponds covering
maybe fifteen acres each. They had their aerators all running—
paddlewheels shoved in the water to churn it around and
sweeten it up so the fish wouldn't suffocate.

"Park it up there." Eugene pointed to a tractor shed beyond
the last pond, and Percy Dwayne pulled in among what
looked like a graveyard of tractor implements. Disk harrows
and cultivators, middle busters and spreaders. There was a
massive combine rusting off to one side.

"Where's the house?" I asked Eugene. He pointed. This

time we'd be wading through soybeans. I could see the sun glinting off a weathered roof just beyond the field.

"Me and you," I told Percy Dwayne. "And don't squeeze off shit unless I say."

"Hear you, boss," Percy Dwayne told me, and off we went into the soybeans with Luther left behind to make sure Eugene and Tommy wouldn't bug out.

We didn't have to worry about reptiles this trip or any living thing. That field had lately been dusted with pesticide or fertilizer or something. The alkaline stink felt like it was drilling a chemical hole in my brain.

"Don't know how I'm going to get all the way over there without breathing."

"What's your trouble?" Percy Dwayne asked me.

"You don't smell that?"

He took a breath so deep it would have sent me straight to the ICU. He shook his head. "Just Delta air," he told me.

I distracted myself from the stink along the way across by checking and rechecking my clips. I kept counting forty rounds, which I took as a sign I was going unscathed, and I was feeling strong and steady until the gunfire started.

It sounded like somebody was shooting at us, that we were downrange of the muzzle anyway, but there weren't any rounds flying by us as best I could tell.

I'd been shot at before by soldiers and civilians, so I knew what it sounded like when somebody was dialing you in. Bullets sing in the air, and when Percy Dwayne and I squatted to listen, we weren't hearing anything but the report.

"Go on?" he asked me.

I nodded. "But stay low."

Of course, that served to make the chemicals that much more undiluted. After another fifty yards, I was half hoping I'd get shot in the head.

There was a silty waste at the fair edge of the field that we scooted across bent low. It ran into a half-assed levee the tractors had pushed up. The thing was maybe five feet tall and meant, I had to guess, to keep the creek beyond it out of the soybeans when it rained.

There'd been a break in the firing, but it picked back up just as we gained the levee. We could both feel the impact as each round struck the dirt. A *thump* and a low vibration. Somebody was taking target practice. We worked down to the left where there were scrubby trees to serve for cover, and I peeked up over the top just as another shot rang out.

There were two guys firing. No-neck endomorphs in track suits. The one with the gauze around his head was Dale.

"I'll be damned," I said. "I knew he was dumb, but I figured he was clean."

Dale was firing what I could tell by the clatter was a Chinese AK knockoff. The eastern bloc ones let go with an intimidating *clunk*, but the Chinese ones sound sort of like a Chinese car door slamming. It's all snap and rattle and imprecision. They don't aim worth a damn, and the recoil tends to break them apart over time.

I motioned for Percy Dwayne to ease up and join me. "Seen them before?" I asked him. The one without the AK was firing what looked to be a Glock. "The one with his head wrapped up is a cop."

"New to me," Percy Dwayne told me. "When Guy showed up at Eugene's and took your car, he had a big blond boy with him. Neal or something. Not either one of them."

I watched as Dale and his buddy let go with a half-dozen rounds, aiming high on the levee where it tapered thin like they were trying to blow a hole clean through. We moved a little further left where the thing was more of a hedgerow than dyke. I glanced back to see that Desmond had already made it over from the Sonic. He was carrying a Sonic sack, red and greasy from the chili, and he was doing his Desmond glide across the field. I was trying to wave him off to the side as those guys opened up again.

I saw Desmond clutch frantically at himself. He performed a pirouette and toppled straight over into the soybeans. I was already scrambling out of the trees and running low across the silt waste when Desmond stood up out of the greenery and waved me off. He kept coming, but he held his right arm as he did, had a hand to the massive hock between his elbow and his shoulder.

"Some fucker shot me," Desmond said as he reached us and pitched his bulk to the ground.

He was bleeding a little between his fingers. I had him take his hand away, and you could see the shank of the bullet sticking out of his bicep.

"The Glock," I told him. "Too far away to go through. You're lucky it wasn't the AK."

"Who the hell are they?"

"Take a look," I said.

Desmond eased around where he could get eyes on those boys. "Is that Dale?"

I nodded. "I'm going to pull this bullet out," I told Desmond, and he explained to me six ways from Sunday exactly why I wouldn't.

That fell in the category of treatment, and Desmond didn't like getting nursed. He wouldn't ever get stitched, wouldn't sit still for vaccinations, had an almost mortal fear of peroxide and rubbing alcohol. The scuffing up never bothered him; it was the doctoring that did him in.

"Bullet's got to come out."

Desmond shook his head. "Leave it for now."

"Where's my Coney Islands?" I asked him.

Desmond motioned with his nose toward the soybeans. "Dropped the bag," he told me. "Kind of landed on it."

As he talked, I pinched that bullet between my forefinger and thumb and plucked it out of Desmond's arm as nice as you please.

"Gawd!" He said it out of reflex. I couldn't have hurt him much.

The wound was a little weepy, but it wasn't really bleeding.

"Hmm," Desmond told me as I handed him the bullet, his version in this circumstance of "thank you very much."

"So what's the deal?" Percy Dwayne asked.

But before I could speak, I heard it and knew instantaneously what it was.

"Listen," I told them both.

A baritone rumble, deep and smooth. I caught a glimpse of the thing piecemeal through the trees. Tropical pink. Polished chrome. It rolled into the clearing unobstructed for a couple of seconds until it got eclipsed by a homely four by four parked out in the yard.

"Damn," Desmond said. "That's a hell of thing."

"Isn't it though?" Percy Dwayne told him.

"You shut up," I advised Percy Dwayne. "We wouldn't be here but for you."

He went sheepish to the extent that Delta trash can manage to seem contrite.

"Who do you see?" I asked him.

Percy Dwayne peered through the foliage with concentration and intent. "No Sissy. No PD," he said, "but that's Guy."

Me and Desmond shifted for a better view and found Guy giving his no-necks hot-headed, psychotic shit. He was in a swivet about something. About his meth houses burning, I guessed. We couldn't exactly hear what he was saying, but it was easy to see that Guy was a fellow who could lay on some scathing abuse.

Anybody with eyes could tell what his trouble was right away. He was one of the wee people. I couldn't have said at the time how tall he was exactly, but he was a head and a half shorter than the guys he was yelling at. They might have been thick and looming, but they weren't exactly giants.

"I get it," I told Desmond. "He's a runt."

Sometimes people explain themselves to you without uttering a word. You can know who they are and what they're made of by looking at them once. I developed a knack for that sort of thing on the PD in Virginia. A civilian would be telling me one thing with his mouth while the rest of him was telling me something else.

Guy was mad he wasn't six foot two, and he expected the world to pay him for it. You could tell it by the way he held himself. You could tell it by the way he screamed, by how he snatched the pistol from the fellow who'd shot Desmond and began to beat him with it while Dale just looked on.

Everything Guy did was ripe with violence and recrimination. And Percy Dwayne was right: He did look a little like a movie star. Mostly because his head was bigger than it needed to be.

He looked to me like a furless Ewok. He was swarthy. Maybe tanned. I couldn't really tell which from where I was. He had his hair slicked back, and he was dressed in the way a fellow like him would think was flashy. He held himself like a rooster on a planet full of hens.

The violence for him, the ghastly, evil bullshit he got up to, was all just compensation for the lifts he needed in his shoes.

He didn't just hit that no-neck once. Guy put him on the ground, and then we watched him beat him with his pistol well after he was down, probably after he was already in a coma. Guy just kept whacking him until he was raising blood and giblets both.

The only move Dale made was to back up and keep clear

of the splatter. He never so much as twitched to suggest he was tempted to intervene.

"Do him," Percy Dwayne suggested.

The thought had more than crossed my mind already. We'd flushed him out like we'd wanted, and I could have gunned him down with ease. But there was something about Guy that told me I just wouldn't be satisfied if all I did was put him in the ground. He'd get the chance to rot there soon enough. He impressed me as the sort who needed to rot a little topside first.

"Shooting's too good for him," I told Percy Dwayne. "I think I need Guy in Parchman for a while. They'll know what to do up there with a fellow who looks like a movie star."

Desmond nodded. Desmond told me, "Yep."

The thing about Guy was that he couldn't seem to get unmad. You'd think a man who'd just beaten a musclehead probably clean to death with a pistol—and not just a couple of blows in the full blush of righteous rage but in a leisurely, attenuated frenzy—would know at least a passing moment of reflection and regret. Even a monster like Jeffrey Dahmer must have paused every now and again, maybe elbow deep in gore, to ask himself, "What the fuck am I up to?"

Guy wasn't even that sensitive. He was simply pissed the way some people are redheads or left-handed.

He finally left off beating his no-neck and flung the Glock onto the ground. He had Dale take his shirt off so he could swab the splatter with it. Then he threw that down too and stalked into the house. We could hear him yelling and banging around in there for a bit as well. When he came back out, he had a few choice words for Dale.

Guy grabbed the Chinese AK out of Dale's hands and fired it like a madman. Straight up in the air. Down into the ground. Swept it along the levee. We couldn't get low enough to feel safe.

He finally emptied the clip and threw the whole damn gun into the woods. He yelled a little more and kept on yelling as he circled around the four by four and climbed into the Ranchero.

I heard that beautiful rumble as he turned the engine over, watched him briefly in the clearing before he reached the trees.

"She look dirty to you?" I asked Desmond, who knew a filthy car when he saw one.

He loosed a mournful snort and told me, "Sure does."

Dale got so busy mourning and poking his colleague with his foot that he didn't see me coming until he'd felt the M4 muzzle in his back.

"Jesus!" was all he said once he'd looked over his shoulder and seen me.

"Moonlighting, Dale?" I asked him as I took his service pistol out of the waistband of his sweats, the very gun I'd taken from his wife not forty-eight hours ago.

"Is he dead?" I asked.

Dale nodded. "But I ain't done it."

"Didn't stop it, either."

Dale started whining about how hard it was to make a

living and how he didn't actually want to be doing what he'd gotten up to, but Guy was a crazy bastard and you couldn't just up and quit him.

Dale seemed to be figuring if he told me he couldn't stand to go to Parchman, I might gun him down just to save him the bother, but if I didn't gun him down, he'd end up locked away for years. It was a bad spot for a fellow to be in, especially a fellow as dumb as Dale who had to labor to weigh out all the possibilities.

Desmond and Percy Dwayne had joined me by then. "Why don't you watch him," I told Desmond. "I'll go in and see what's what."

I handed him Dale's 9 mm and Desmond hit him with it.

"I don't like getting shot," Desmond told Dale.

Dale told Desmond, "Ow!"

Me and Percy Dwayne went inside. This house wasn't like the other places. It was furnished and homey, and there were three Mexicans at the kitchen table weighing out the meth they'd made.

They could just as well have been making tamales to sell to the restaurant trade. The house was that clean and orderly, and none of those three boys looked like users. They even got a little jolly once we'd convinced them in broken Spanish that they weren't about to be dead.

We took the drugs in a gym duffel. I figured we might have use for them, and I told those Mexicans to clear out. Then me and Percy Dwayne went back out to join Desmond.

"That yours?" I asked Dale of the Tahoe in the yard.

He nodded.

"Not anymore."

I gave it to the Mexicans, told them to drive Dale home. We trussed him up with a length of clothesline and loaded him in the way back.

"Don't go anywhere," I told Dale. "Don't talk to anybody. We'll find you in a while."

He nodded. He was hardly having the week he'd hoped to have.

Those three Mexicans piled into the four by four and headed down the track. Me and Desmond and Percy Dwayne carried Dale's dead colleague into the house. We left his bloody Glock on the floor right beside him.

We didn't light this one, left it just like it had been. We crossed back through the soybeans with their agrichemical stink. Blue sky. High clouds. An acrobatic Ag Cat on the horizon.

TWENTY-THREE

Eugene was finished. I didn't need Luther to tell me that. Eugene was like a child who sits down in the trail and won't go on. He was drained and spent, and I let him uncork a litany of every damn thing he wouldn't do no matter how I tried to make him.

"Fine," I told him. "You and him go on home."

Tommy hadn't even started to tell me what I couldn't make him be up to, but I had to think him and Eugene were on the same page.

"Sure about this, boss?" Luther asked me.

I nodded. "It doesn't matter anymore. There's nothing they can say. Nobody they can tell. Send them back to the swamp. We'll find Guy's hunting lodge without them."

"Well, you're welcome all to hell." Eugene didn't quite have indignation down, but he made a decent show of being offended.

"Your choice," I told him. "I can't help it if you miss your cut."

"What cut?" Eugene asked me.

"What do you think'll become of that money if we leave it to the cops?"

"Fuckers'll steal it," Luther declared.

And Desmond added, "Fuckers will."

"He's up by Blue Hole," Eugene announced. "And I don't go unless I drive."

So it was lumpy backroads all the way over from Louise to Anguilla, up through Booth and Grace and over to Addie and then down on the Blue Hole road. I quizzed Eugene along the way to find out what we might run into. From what I'd seen of Guy and what I could believe from Eugene, the man ran too hot to be careful. That's why he'd had to leave New Orleans at a sprint.

He was throttled up all the time and didn't know how to dial it back. He was his own security force, couldn't trust anybody else to do the job. Neal was just a living gun rack who fetched him shit and took abuse. That could work to our advantage. Guy didn't have a loyal crew, just boys getting paid to hang around and suffer his abuse. Guy seemed to have decided he was too notorious for anybody to touch him, so famously crazy that nobody would have the stones to take him down. Burn a few houses maybe but never seek him in his lair.

Blue Hole was one of those cutout lakes that the river had left when it wandered. It was a tiny one as those things go, maybe forty acres at most. The terrain around it was all marshy except for a half mile or so of compacted silt between the lake and the river. The land was thick with cypress and cotton-woods, and Guy's was the only structure for miles.

He had a gate with an intercom halfway down what proved to be his driveway and a run of fencing either side that simply petered out in the scrub. It was just the sort of half-assed compound a psychotic Acadian fuck stick would build. You walked around a little one way or the other and you were in.

We got to where we could see the roofline before we stopped to make some sort of plan.

"One thing," I said after we'd decided who'd go where and how. "It'd be a lot better if we didn't have to kill him." Of course, I was talking to Percy Dwayne. "You can scuff him up if you need to, but short of making him dead. We've got to look out for your wife and baby. They're in there somewhere, too."

We all went in, even Eugene and Tommy. They weren't laying back if there was money involved. We spread out and slipped up from tree to tree, from grassy hummock to hum-mock.

It was moccasin country and gator terrain, so we had a lot to think about. The Ranchero was parked up under the house. There was a truck in the yard and a Blazer, and even before I could see him, I could hear Guy screaming at some-body about something.

The house was up out of the swamp on stilts, and the deck wrapped full around it. It was little short of palatial compared to Eugene's. A Mississippi version of a chalet.

Guy wandered into view. He was stalking along the deck, circling the house and talking on his phone. He was pissed, of course, but I couldn't quite make out who he was pissed at or why. He was wearing just briefs, black Calvins, and he had a green bath towel draped around his neck. He didn't have any muscle with him. Just him in his underwear, strutting around like he was bulletproof.

Every time he wandered out of sight, I moved a little closer until I was twenty yards or so from the south end of the place. Guy came around again, still irate. He was yelling at a plumber. He'd been in the shower—washing the blood and the giblets away, I guess—when the drainpipe had backed up. He kept wondering if that plumber had ever been ankle-deep in shit.

As propositions go, that one seemed pretty likely to me, but Guy couldn't get an answer he was happy with. So he barked a little louder, which apparently was his lone method and technique.

Me and Desmond were the first ones under the place, which was about where our plan gave out. You couldn't really plan on storming a house you'd never laid eyes on before and calculate how to keep yourself from getting blown to pieces. So we were just standing there trying between us to work up the adrenaline to go up and in, when Percy Dwayne and Luther joined us by the pilings and started to press us on the plan we didn't have.

Then we all heard that Vardaman's voice, a little muffled from upstairs, and me and Desmond had to sit on Percy Dwayne to hold him where he was. Luther, his nephew, kicked him a little, which wasn't terribly helpful.

Eugene and Tommy were stuck behind a cypress tree and had decided they were comfortable a good fifty yards from the house, particularly once they'd spotted us all wrestling under the decking. We very nearly had to cut off Percy Dwayne's air to calm him down. It helped when Guy got on the phone again since he was loud and strenuous about it. We were able to convince Percy Dwayne that Guy couldn't likely rage on the phone and ravish Sissy all at once.

Guy was yelling at a second plumber. The first one must have blown him off, evidence of the limits of being furious all the time. It only barely works on people in your actual employ. The razor-sharp Japanese blade tends to help, along with the willingness to use it. But some jobber over in Yazoo City with plenty of other plumbing to fix?

The more I listened to Guy, the lower he fell in my esteem. He was one note only. There wasn't a wise or subtle thing about him.

"He's an idiot," I told Desmond. "Just a hothead with no brakes."

Desmond nodded. Desmond told me, "Yep."

Because the drain was backed up, nobody could use the toilets in the house. This proved to be a special problem for Neal, Guy's pumped-up bodyguard. It turned out he'd built his muscles at the general expense of his bladder.

We heard him on the deck, clumping along. While Guy kept circulating and yelling, Neal headed for the stairs that went down toward a swampy eddy behind the house. He had a Tec 9 hanging on a strap around his neck and a Sig Pro in a holster on his hip. He also had such an urgent need to take a leak that he was entirely oblivious to us lurking behind the pilings.

Lucky for us, the stairs were a straight run down from top to bottom, and Neal stepped off the last tread with his back to us and wandered out to the edge of the marsh to pee. Guy was still yelling overhead, which was helpful.

He was a do-you-know-who-I-am sort of guy in a place where nobody gives a happy shit who you are. It was a tough go for him. Most Delta plumbers don't need a meth-slinging Acadian fuck stick to help them make their nut. Guy was learning that the hard way and taking his sweet time doing it.

So there wasn't any mystery where Guy was from one second to the next. Neal had whipped out his shriveled member and was poisoning the swamp when I gave Luther the nod, and he slipped out with his Taser. Guy was on the far end being irate when Luther went down on one knee like a big game hunter and fired his darts right into Neal's back.

I think Neal electrified the marsh there for a second. Desmond has always insisted he saw sparks. All I know is Neal just kept on peeing for a while and then finally fell over and peed a little bit more. Me and Desmond eased out to drag him under before Guy came around on his circuit. It sounded like another plumber was explaining that yes, in fact, he had stood ankle-deep in shit before.

The landing party was me and Desmond with Percy Dwayne bringing up the rear. We eased up those back stairs while Guy yelled from the far end of the house. I sent Desmond around to the left, and I went the other way with Percy Dwayne and K-Lo's Beretta behind me. Guy was bound to run from one of us right into the other's sights.

Then something altogether too Mississippi happened. Guy's second plumber hung up on him, and Guy said a few goddamns but fell silent right as me and Desmond were about to close and nab him. There was a lull while Guy tried (I guess) to figure who he ought to call and scream at next, and that's when we all heard Eugene tell Tommy, "Was a goddamn spinner with Baitmate."

Those two swamp rats were arguing lures again. It wasn't much to hear, but it was enough.

I heard Guy say, "Shit!" followed by his rapid footfall on the decking.

Desmond must have heard him too because we both came charging from opposite sides of the house and caught a glimpse of Guy as he ducked in through a doorway.

"Aw hell," I remember thinking, and then charged straight in behind him.

He was pawing on the couch for something, so I fired a burst over his head. I heard a woman scream from somewhere back down the hall and a baby cry, which was enough to put me off of gunplay.

Guy went dodging away empty handed as Desmond came in through the door behind me.

I could see now Guy wasn't just in his underwear, but he was oily, too. So while I didn't want to shoot him necessarily, I certainly didn't want to tussle with him.

There wasn't much danger of that, as it turned out, because he was a quick little son of a bitch. I blocked off the way to the outside door. Desmond closed off the back hallway, and we took turns trying to close in on him and maybe knock him down.

It was like chasing a squirrel barehanded, and then he fetched his knife from somewhere. That big shiny Japanese thing he'd been looking for all along. You could tell he loved that blade. It was oiled and honed and sang when he whipped it through the air.

So it was still like chasing a squirrel but now a squirrel with a machete. If we hadn't much wanted to lay hands on him before, we really didn't want to now.

Desmond was begging me to let him shoot Guy. "I ain't even fired my gun."

"Can you hit him in the leg?"

"If he'll hold still a little."

"I don't see that happening."

And all of this was transpiring while Guy was telling us how dead we were about to be and asking if we had any idea just who the fuck he was. He was laughing and wild-eyed and kept darting at us swinging that Japanese knife.

"You know who I am?" he'd say every time he made a

lunge, and me and Desmond would take turns telling him he was a crazy Acadian fuck stick.

We were about decided we'd have to shoot him when he made a move toward the window. Guy sliced out the screen like Zorro would have, just made a swipe and it was gone. He had a little more to tell us about the shit storm we'd be seeing, and then took a run up and tried to dive outside head first.

He didn't, as it turned out, go anywhere at all. It was a shocking thing to watch. Me and Desmond heard a sickening *thunk*, and then Guy fell back inside.

He dropped to the floor in a heap. That knife came clattering down on top of him without slicing, as luck would have it, anything important off. Guy's head bounced off the planking. His breath departed him entirely. He was just about as precipitously senseless as a human will ever get.

It turned out Guy had run cranium first into the butt of K-Lo's Beretta. Percy Dwayne had caught him a full thrusting blow flush on the top of his head.

Percy Dwayne peered in through the window. "SISSY!" was all he said.

He came scrabbling in over the sill, and we went searching around the house. Percy Dwayne's wife and his boy were shut up together in a back bedroom. That child looked to be wearing the same diaper I'd met him in two days before. He was fragrant and unhappy, and Percy Dwayne took him from his wife and handed him to me. I'd almost rather have wrestled with Guy, Japanese knife or not.

"Give us a minute?" Percy Dwayne said, and me and

Desmond and that smelly child retired into the front room while Percy Dwayne and his Vardaman wife had a bit of a chat. It was lively and loud. She claimed to have been there to steal money all along.

"I did it for us," was her refrain throughout.

She said she'd packed some cash away in little PD's diaper, and Percy Dwayne came into the front room to have a look. Sure enough there were four thousand dollars worth of twenties in his pants in wet bundles that looked, for all the world, like they had been chocolate frosted.

You could see Percy Dwayne change at the sight of that cash. It was like watching ice melt in an oven. In seconds he went from hurt and irritated all the way to proud. Desmond and me were both stuck at disgusted, chiefly on account of the stink and the frosted money.

"You were working him," Percy Dwayne said to his wife with both wonderment and hunger.

She nodded and assured him, "I sure was."

They fell together and went tonsil deep. Since Guy was still out cold, I sat the baby on the floor, and me and Desmond went exploring.

Guy didn't have a money room exactly. He had a money closet. It was equipped with a bill counter and a box of bands, trunks to keep the cash in. And there was an awful lot of cash, five or six hundred thousand dollars, probably. We didn't trouble ourselves to count it. We even left a little in the closet so they could find some after the fire.

By the time we got down on the ground with Guy, Eugene

and Tommy had come out of the marsh and had joined Luther under the house. They were still quarreling a little about how big a sturgeon can actually get, but the sight of Guy unconscious and stretched out in his briefs undid them.

"I thought the fucker would kill you," Eugene told me.

"He gave it a shot," I said, and I handed Eugene the Japanese knife that I'd carried with me down the stairs.

"It's nice and all," he said, "but I hope this ain't my cut."

We shoved Neal into the Blazer and drove it out clear of the house. He would wake up and get away or not. It hardly mattered to us. We taped up Guy, wrapped him in a bedsheet, and put him in the bed of Gil's calypso coral Ranchero. Proof that it could haul something after all.

Only then did we divide up the money, essentially by weight. Five shares. Eugene and Tommy got one to split. Percy Dwayne and his people got another. Me and Luther and Desmond each took a share for ourselves. I didn't have to say anything about not spending it all at once and drawing unwelcome attention from precisely the wrong people. The Delta is as tight as Glasgow. They'd be squeezing those bills until they screamed.

"Want a truck?" I asked Percy Dwayne, and he loaded his family up in Guy's Tundra. Luther crawled in, too, and they invited Eugene and Tommy into the bed so they could drop them where we'd parked up past the gate.

"Well," Percy Dwayne said, and the rest of them added some variation on it. Then Percy Dwayne pulled away, and

they were gone on up the drive. No fond good-byes. No broth-
erly hugs. Just a little spit out the side windows.

That's what I like about Delta crackers—they're only
sentimental about their mommas. If anybody ever tells you
different, it's a lie.

Me and Desmond set the house ablaze and watched it burn
for a little while. We'd seen enough houses on fire by then to
be a little weary of it. We left once the place was going hard,
and I dropped Desmond at his Metro. Guy had woken up and
was stirring in the bed, wiggling under the sheet. I fetched the
fireplace shovel off of Desmond's floorboard. It only took one
whack, and not even a firm one, to put Guy back to sleep.

I followed Desmond up 61. He went cross-country near
Estill, and we passed into Sunflower County on the old
Klinock Road. A few miles south of Indianola, a fellow had
junked a spreader truck. Weeds had grown up all around it. It
wasn't ten feet from the ditch.

We put Guy in the cab, taped his hands to the steering
wheel. He was coming around again by then. We set the duffel full of crystal meth on the truck seat right beside him.

"Call Dale," I told Desmond. "Kendell, too. Tell them
there's some fellow with a bunch of drugs out here in a truck.
Let's see who gets here first."

Guy woke up pissed, of course. He glanced around in the
failing light at the gym bag alongside him. He seemed to have
a fair sense of what we were about and where he'd probably
end up.

He rocked and lurched and tried to pull loose, called us all sorts of things, which we couldn't make out because of the tape on his pie hole.

"Vamos?" I asked Desmond.

Desmond nodded, and we both told Guy the Acadian fuck stick, "Adios, buddy."

TWENTY-FOUR

I went straight to the Magic Wand and gave Gil's Ranchero a bath. A half a bath really, because while I had a hundred odd thousand dollars, hardly any of it was in change. It looked good, though. That Ranchero was so simonized all over, it was virtually impervious to dirt. I drove it around for another half hour just to let it dry. That's what I told myself I was up to, anyway. I don't think I ever entirely lifted my hand from the walnut gearshift knob.

It was past eight by the time I pulled into Pearl's driveway, and she came out expecting a party. I don't believe she even noticed what I'd arrived in at first.

"Where are your friends?" she asked me.

"Back home," I said. "Probably won't be around for a bit."

"Oh." Pearl's tone was ripe with disappointment.

"But look." I was obliged to point out the Ranchero.

She told me just "Oh" again.

She was so crestfallen after two nights of spontaneous dinner parties that I would have packed her into Gil's Ranchero and taken her out for a meal, but there wasn't much of anywhere to go unless you were craving chicken nuggets or a fisherman's platter that hadn't seen salt water in a while.

"I could stand some scrambled eggs," I told her.

"Well come on, then," she said, lifted a little.

"You heat up a pan. I'm right behind you."

I took my share of the money into Pearl's basement, down her outside steps and through the back door. I packed it among the boxes and the cartons that had accumulated on the dry end of the cellar where the rain didn't seep in and the water heater didn't leak.

Pearl was at the stove melting aged, discolored oleo in a skillet by the time I arrived in the kitchen. She asked after Desmond and all of my cracker friends in turn, and I concocted details and circumstances like we were all upstanding people with regular lives and responsibilities and decent motives at heart. Then I managed to get a name from Pearl of a doctor for Desmond's mom.

"Here's the thing," I told her once I was sitting at the dining room table pushing eggs around my plate with a scrap of moldy toast. "I'd like to buy Gil's Ranchero. I'd love it like he did. I think it means more to me already than any car ever has."

Pearl drove a silver Buick that she'd dinged up every-where. She looked at me as if she found me ever so slightly demented. "Really?"

"Yes, ma'am."

"That'd make Gil happy," she said.

I glanced at the snapshot of Gil over on Pearl's sideboard. In his immaculate coveralls. Armor All-ing a tire. I doubted "happy" really figured in.

Pearl had come across one of Gil's key fobs in a junky kitchen drawer. It was an old Ford logo stamped in metal in a mildewed leather frame. I fixed the Ranchero key to it straightaway, went up to my apartment over the car shed, threw open the windows to help get the unwashed and un-laundered man stink out, fell into bed, and passed out like I'd been beat with a shovel.

K-Lo didn't know we were coming until me and Desmond just showed up. We'd laid out a few more days because we were weary and could afford to. The K-Lo we found wasn't overhauled exactly, but he was certainly altered a little. Get-ting his bobcat back had sure helped things along. I can't conceive that it's in people for them to simply up and change, but K-Lo was hardly so sharp around the edges as he'd been. Mostly elbows still but not elbows entirely.

K-Lo made a show for the rest of the crew out on the sales floor. He berated me and Desmond for going AWOL on him, and we made an attempt to be suitably contrite. I brought K-Lo's Beretta in through the back door and what was left of his box of shells, didn't want anybody to get the impression that K-Lo would loan stuff out. I paid the money I'd borrowed, returning it in twenties with interest.

Back in his office, K-Lo showed us a fresh copy of the Sunflower County *Enterprise-Tocsin* with a photo of Dale and a table full of Baggies right there on the front page. Dale, it appeared, had raced out and gotten to that fuck stick first.

The article that went with the photo ran for a column on the front and finished on an inside back page between a tire ad and the weekly affirmation. It was largely fiction, particularly the parts that made Dale out to be capable and dogged and honest.

"You working or not?" K-Lo asked us.

We glanced at each other, me and Desmond. We hadn't thought about it much. Hadn't discussed it at all. That's what happens to you when you come home with a box of money.

"A little, I guess," I told K-Lo.

Desmond nodded and said, "Yep."

"Go talk to these people about their TV," K-Lo said. "See if you can make it all right." He offered us a tissuey pink invoice.

I ended up helping Desmond carry his mother to the medical complex. She wasn't hinged anymore in a fashion that would allow her to fit in the Geo. We got her in my Ranchero and I drove her across town.

"Complex" was a little ambitious. It was an office with a breezeway to another office that hadn't been built yet. Pearl's doctor determined that Desmond's momma had a plumbing problem. Not so simple a one as Guy's had been but fixable nonetheless. Beyond that, of course, she also had an OxyContin problem, which Desmond sent her for a month to a niece's up in Oak Park to address. She got off the pills by getting on the Yellow Tail instead.

Guy, for his part, didn't choose to bother with a trial. He spun some wild story about a crazy cracker bastard and a black guy half again as big as a cow. The meth was all theirs. They'd just trussed him up and dumped it on him. Worse still, the cop that had found him was as dirty as the day is long.

Dale didn't remember it quite that way. He'd done a fair bit of subduing. That the Acadian fuck stick had put up a fight was clear enough from Dale's injuries. Then there was the body police had been put onto over near Louise. Some lowlife from Jackson who appeared to have been throttled to death with a pistol. The nickel-plated Glock found on the floor alongside him had Guy's fingerprints all over it in blood.

At his allocution, Guy tried to rant about one thing and another, but the judge gaveled him hard and shut him down. Guy threw up his shackled hands and said, "What's the fucking use?"

Me and Desmond had come for the show and were sitting in the back of the courtroom. Dale was up front in his dress uniform with Patty at his side. Guy didn't give a rat's ass about him, but when me and Desmond rose together to make sure he saw us, it took three bailiffs to finally knock him over and hold him down.

I had to figure he'd make the sort of friends during his stay in Parchman who'd have an interest in his drainpipe and wouldn't give a shit who he was.

We capped the day off with steaks at Luscos over on the far side of Greenwood. We drove there in Desmond's spanking new, resplendent Escalade.

I didn't keep up with Percy Dwayne and Luther, though I saw them once at a traffic light. I was over by Greenville where the truck route crosses Highway 1, and they eased up beside me and blew the horn. Percy Dwayne was still driving Guy's Tundra. He'd get caught in it or not.

Angie came down, and we hunted ducks. That's what we called it, anyway. We sat on a blanket in the sun over by Tarpley Neck, on a little rise from where we could see the Mississippi. We drank wine all afternoon and didn't talk about anything much. We were easy enough together that we didn't actually need to talk.

I had Angie get in touch with Pearl's worthless son in New Orleans so I could offer him five hundred dollars to spend a weekend with his mom. I'd never seen Pearl prouder. She even got to nurse him a little once her outdated dingy mayonnaise very nearly did him in.

Pearl was so delighted that I negotiated Christmas for an even thousand. Little of my life felt different, but nothing was the same. I didn't have frets and worries. I worked for K-Lo when I wanted, and it turned out I wanted almost all the time. The change was largely internal, but I couldn't quite put it into words. I didn't have to, in the end, because Desmond did it for me.

"When you've got money," Desmond told me one day in between Coney Islands, "everything slows down."

That was it, and we were living already in the slowest place on earth. Time in the Delta is measured in agriculture. Fertile and fallow. Deluge and drought. Seed and harvest. About the only monotony breaker was a car that would go fast. I had one, so it was only a matter of time before Kendell snared me.

I was watching a crop duster on a back road between Rising Sun and Quito. Those pilots are all about half crazy— flying twelve feet off the ground, dodging power lines and hedgerows, threatening a stall with every turn. He swept around so tight his wings went perpendicular to the ground.

His Ag Cat was yellow and looked freshly painted. I could barely take my eyes off the thing. It hardly mattered to me, in the Delta way, that I was doing eighty.

Apparently, it mattered to Kendell. He was behind me for a while before I glanced at my rearview mirror and saw his beacon. Kendell gave me a yelp on his siren and pointed up ahead toward a dirt tract that bisected a cotton field.

I pulled in. He pulled in behind me. I was out of the Ranchero and leaning on the fender when Kendell finally climbed from his cruiser and walked up. He hadn't bothered to bring his summons book.

"Don't think I don't know what you did," Kendell said.

Together we watched that Ag Cat swoop and glide. "You and Desmond and them other fellows."

Kendell's not the sort I'd want to insult with a lie. So I just stood there and didn't say a thing.

"I talked to Calvin," he told me.

I had to think back. "Dashiki," I said.

Kendell nodded. "He gave me a fair idea of what's what."

"Keep an eye on Dale," I told him.

"Doing it already," Kendell said.

We watched that Ag Cat bank into a roll as it swooped out over the blacktop.

"Fool," he muttered. About the pilot. Maybe me. Possibly both.

"Tell me this," I said to Kendell. "Am I making you tired?"

"Maybe," he allowed, "a little at the edges." Then he took a moment to study my Ranchero from end to end. "Nice . . . uh . . . car," he told me.

Kendell went back to his cruiser and whipped out onto the pavement, flinging gravel. I stayed where I was and watched that lunatic pilot finish his work.

Once he'd sprayed the last rows, he banked my way and came screaming directly at me, probably not more than twenty feet off the ground. He passed over in a yellow flash. I could see him beneath the canopy. He was grinning. He was upside down.